Quick Tips to Form an English Sentence

英語句型

這樣學才會快

國家圖書館出版品預行編目資料

英語句型這樣學才會快 / 范欣楣著
-- 初版 -- 新北市：雅典文化，民110. 02
面 ; 公分. -- (全民學英文 ; 59)
ISBN 978-986-99431-4-7(平裝附光碟片)

1. 英語　　2. 句法

805. 169　　　　　　　　　　109021243

全民學英文系列 59

英語句型這樣學才會快

著／范欣楣
責任編輯／張文娟
美術編輯／鄭孝儀
封面設計／林鈺恆

法律顧問：方圓法律事務所／涂成樞律師

總經銷：永續圖書有限公司
永續圖書線上購物網
www.foreverbooks.com.tw

出版日／2021年02月

雅典文化

出版社

22103　新北市汐止區大同路三段194號9樓之1
TEL　(02) 8647-3663
FAX　(02) 8647-3660

CONTENTS

1 轉折連結

CONTENTS

② 表達疑問

CONTENTS

CONTENTS

❸ 表達情緒

CONTENTS

4 表達否定

CONTENTS

5 生活用語

CONTENTS

CONTENTS

CONTENTS

CONTENTS

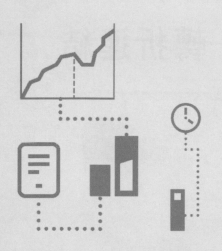

Chapter 1

轉折連結

001

★ A and B...

A 和 B...

完整句型為 A and B+V(複數的be動詞或一般動詞)。此句中的and連接A還有B，屬於對等連接詞的概念，所以A若是名詞，B也必須是名詞，其詞性或屬性必須相同，例如：My dad and my mom....(我爸和我媽...)或是Dogs and cats....(狗和貓...)。

例 Kelly and Kate are my friends.
凱莉和凱特是我的朋友。

例 My sister and I like movies.
我妹妹和我喜歡電影。

例 Jim and Jack walk home every day.
吉姆和傑克每天走路回家。

例 Fried chicken and hamburgers are fast food.
炸雞和漢堡是速食。

★ A... but B...

A...但 B...

完整句型為 A+V(動詞),but B+V(動詞)。這裡的 but 連接 A 和 B,雖然中間有個 but,不過它仍屬於對等連接詞,所以 A 和 B 的詞性也要相同。而句中的逗點可有可無,視句子的長短而定。

例 I like black but he likes white.
　　我喜歡黑色,但他喜歡白色。

例 She is short but she runs fast.
　　她個子小但卻跑得快。

例 I want to go home but I can't.
　　我想回家但是我無法回家。

例 He is short but he is very strong.
　　他個子雖矮卻很強壯。

★ A or B...

A 或 B.../...否則...

❶ 轉折連結

❷ 表達疑問

❸ 表達情緒

❹ 表達否定

❺ 生活用語

用法

完整句型可為 A or B, S+V.、A or B+V.、S+V A or B.或為 S1+V1 or S2+V2。所以 or 的位置無論放在哪裡，皆是連接兩個相提並論的事物(可為兩個名詞或是兩個句子)。

例句

例 This one or that one, pick one.

這一個或是那一個，選一個。

例 Hurry up, or we will be late!

快點，不然我們會遲到！

例 You or I have to do it now.

你或我必須現在就去做。

例 Adam never drinks or smokes.

亞當從不喝酒或抽菸。

004

★ Although S+V...

雖然...

 用法

完整句型為Although S+V, S+V.而此句中的兩個
主詞S可為同一人或不同人,須視說話者的內容
而定。另外,中文常講「雖然...但是...」,不過
要注意的是,although和but不能放在同一句子
裡,只能選其一。

 例句

🔠 Although he is poor, he is happy.
雖然他很窮,卻很快樂。

🔠 Although she looks ugly, she is nice.
雖然她看起來很醜,但人卻很好。

🔠 Although Helen eats a lot, she looks thin.
雖然海倫吃很多,她看起來還是瘦的。

🔠 Although the work is hard, I won't give up.
雖然這工作很難,但我不會放棄。

★ As a result, S+V...

結果...

用法

完整句型為As a result, S+V.但也可為S+V, as a result, S+V.(這裡的S主詞可為同一人或不同人)。從句中可知as a result可放句首或句中,若置於句中,則要加上逗點。as a result是連接詞,可用來連接兩個句子。

例句

例 As a result, he got fired.
結果,他被解雇了。

例 As a result, George forgot his book.
結果,喬治忘了他的書。

例 As a result, she lost the game.
結果,她輸了這場比賽。

例 He was too tired,as a result, he didn't go out.
他太累了,所以他沒有外出。

006

🎧track 1-3

★ As long as S+V...

只要...

 用法

完整句型可為 As long as S+V, S+V.或為 S+V, as long as S+V.句中的 as long as 屬於連接詞,主要用來連接兩個句子,可放句首或句中。

例句

例 As long as you finish your homework, you can watch TV.

只要你完成功課就可以看電視。

例 As long as you work hard, you will succeed.

只要你努力,就會成功。

例 As long as I pass the test, I can get the job.

只要我通過該測驗,就能得到這工作。

例 I will let you go, as long as you tell the truth.

我會讓你走,只要你說實話。

 034

★ As soon as S+V...

當...

用法

完整句型為 As soon as S+V, S+V.這裡的S可為同
一人或不同人，須視說話者所表達的意思而定。
這裡的as soon as就等於when。

例句

例 As soon as you see Leo, please call me.
當你見到李奧時，請打給我。

例 As soon as her mom left, she cried.
當她媽媽一走，她就哭了。

例 As soon as I come home, I will take a shower.
我一回家就去洗澡。

例 As soon as I leave home, I will turn off the light.
我一離開家就會關燈。

0 3 5

❶ 轉折連結

❷ 表達疑問

❸ 表達情緒

❹ 表達否定

❺ 生活用語

008

 track 1-4

★ Because of+N, S+V...

因為...

用法

完整句型為Because of + N(名詞), S+V.句中的
because和of連用時，後面一定要加名詞，而非句
子。只有在Because S+V, S+V這樣的句型中，單
用because才可加上句子，作為連接詞之用。但其
實兩種句型所表達之意皆同，只是寫法不同。

例句

例 Because of your help, I got a job.
因為你的幫忙，我找到了工作。

例 Because of Sarah, Ted changed a lot.
因為莎拉的緣故，泰德改變了許多。

例 Because of the rain, we cancelled the game.
因為下雨，我們取消了比賽。

例 Because of the storm, we couldn't find Karen.
因為這場暴風雨，我們找不到凱倫。

★ Besides, S+V...

除此之外...

用法

完整句型可為 Besides, S+V.或為 besides + N(名詞), S+V.前者的 besides 當作副詞，後者則為介係詞(介係詞後面要加名詞)，例如：Besides reading, I also like music.(除了閱讀以外，我還喜歡音樂。)

例句

例 Besides, I still have lots of things to do.
除此之外，我還有許多事要處理。

例 Besides, I want you to promise me one thing.
除此之外，我還要你答應我一件事。

例 Besides, she has to take care of her mom.
除此之外，她還得照顧她媽媽。

例 Besides, we need to finish the work before tomorrow.
除此之外，我們要在明天之前完成這項工作。

❶ 轉折連結
❷ 表達疑問
❸ 表達情緒
❹ 表達否定
❺ 生活用語

010

★ between A and B...

在 **A** 和 **B** 之間...

用法

完整句型為 S+V between A and B.也可為 Between
A and B, S+V.這裡的 between 置於句中時,不用
加逗點。此外,between 只能介於兩者(兩個名詞)
之間,不能超過兩個名詞。

例句

例 His age is between 35 and 40.
他的年齡介於35歲到40歲之間。

例 My home is between the park and the
school.
我家位於那座公園和學校之間。

例 Jess sits between Mark and Nick.
傑斯坐在馬克和尼克之間。

例 There is a bridge between the city and
the town.
在那座城市和小鎮之間,有一座橋。

★ But for+N, S+V...

要不是...

用法

完整句型為 But for +N, S+V.也可為S+V, but for + N.句中的but for只能加名詞,不能加句子,位置可在句首或句中。這裡的but for是一種假設語氣,因此後面的動詞型態須視說話者所要表達之意來調整。常用的動詞型態為 would / could / might + V(原形),或是 would / could / might + have Vpp(分詞)。

例句

📙 But for you, I wouldn't be here.
要不是你,我現在就不會在這裡。

📙 But for her help, I wouldn't succeed.
要不是有她的幫忙,我現在不會成功。

📙 But for the meeting, I wouldn't meet my wife.
要不是那場會議,我現在就不會認識我的老婆。

📙 But for his hard work, he would have failed.
要不是他有努力工作,他早就失敗了。

★ By the time S+V...

在...之前...

完整句型為 By the time S1+V1, S2+V2 因為 by the time連接兩個有先後順序之意的句子，所以在 By the time S1+V1, S2+V2 的句型中，S2+V2 為較早發生的情況，因此V2的動詞型態通常是以 had+Vpp(分詞)過去完成式來表示，而V1則是簡單過去式。

例 By the time he came home, we had left.
在他到家之前，我們早就離開了。

例 By the time we arrived, the train had gone.
在我們到達之前，火車早就已經開走。

例 By the time you told me the news, I had known it.
在你告訴我這消息之前，我早已知道了。

例 By the time we called the police, the thief had disappeared.
在我們報警之前，小偷早已消聲匿跡了。

★ Consequently, S+V...

因此...

用法

完整句型為Consequently,S+V.或為S+V and
consequently S+V.這裡的consequently當作副詞，
放句首時，其後可直接加上完整的句子；若想用
來連接兩個動詞或句子，則須加上and。例如：
I'm busy and consequently I can't talk to you now.
(我在忙，因此我現在無法跟你談話。)

例句

例 Consequently, I need to go home now.
   因此，我現在必須馬上回家。

例 Consequently, I can't go to your birthday
   party.
   因此，我無法參加你的生日派對。

例 Consequently, I was late for work.
   因此，我上班遲到了。

例 Consequently, they won the game.
   因此，他們贏得了比賽。

❶ 轉折連結　❷ 表達疑問　❸ 表達情緒　❹ 表達否定　❺ 生活用語

014

🎧 track 1-7

★ Even if S+V...

即使...

用法

完整句型為Even if S1+V1, S2+V2 這裡的even if 可當作條件句或假設句。若當條件句用，Even if S1+V1, S2+V2 中的V1 則為現在簡單式，V2 則可為現在簡單式或未來式。若為假設句使用的話，V1 為過去簡單式，V2 就為 would /should /could / might +V(原形)，此情況為"與現在事實相反"。V1 為 had+Vpp, V2 則為 would /should /could /might +have Vpp，此情況為"與過去事實相反"。

例句

例 Even if it rains, we will go out.
即使下雨，我們還是要出去。

例 Even if he is poor, she loves him.
即使他很窮，她還是愛他。

例 Even if we don't have money, we will finish it.
即使我們沒有錢，我們還是要把它完成。

例 Even if the challenge is difficult, Ben won't give up, either.
即使這挑戰很艱難，班也不會放棄。

① 轉折連結
② 表達疑問
③ 表達情緒
④ 表達否定
⑤ 生活用語

★ Even S+V...

甚至...

用法

完整句型為Even S+V.或為S+V, even +比較級形容詞，例如：Mike is very tall, even taller than his dad.(麥克很高，甚至比他爸還高。)

例句

例 Even the kid knew the answer.
連那個小孩子都知道答案。

例 Even my dad cried.
連我爸爸都哭了。

例 Even Carol moved away.
甚至凱若都搬走了。

例 Even Sam failed the test.
甚至連山姆都考不及格了。

★ Even though S+V...

雖然...

用法

> 完整句型為 Even though S+V, S+V.句中的 even
> though 等同於 although 以及 though，皆表示 "雖
> 然" 之意，因此其用法也相同，屬於連接詞，且
> 不可和 but 並用在同一句子中。

例句

例 Even though he is fat, he runs very fast.
雖然他胖，但他跑得很快。

例 Even though she doesn't like English, she learns it.
雖然她不喜歡英文，但她還是去學。

例 Even though I want to see the movie, I don't have time.
雖然我想去看電影，但是我沒有時間。

例 Even though you don't like the work, you must do it.
雖然你不喜歡這工作，但你還是得做。

★ Every time S+V...

每一次...

完整句型為Every time S+V,S+V.這裡的every time
要分開，可用來連接兩個句子。

例 Every time Ryan wins the game.
每一次萊恩都贏得比賽。

例 Every time he sees Kelly, he feels happy.
每一次他看到凱莉，他就覺得很開心。

例 Every time she hears the voice, she gets
angry.
每一次她聽見那個聲音，她就會生氣。

例 Every time Amy comes home late, mom
looks worried.
每一次艾咪晚回家，媽看起來就是一臉擔心的樣子。

★ except+N...

除此以外...

完整句型為Except + N,S+V.或為S+V, except + N. 這裡的except表示"除了...以外,再也沒有...", 與besides表示"除了...以外,還有...",兩者意 思不同,在此需要特別注意。

例 Except the news, I don't know others.
除了這消息以外,我不知道其他的。

例 Except Mark, I don't have any friends.
除了馬克以外,我沒有任何朋友。

例 The store opens every day, except Monday.
除了星期一以外,那家店每天都有開。

例 No one knows my real name, except you.
除了你以外,沒人知道我的真實姓名。

★ Finally, S+V...

最後;終於...

用法

完整句型為Finally, S+V.或為S+V finally.也可為 S+ finally +V.由此三種句型可知,finally當作副詞,所以其位置可說是相當彈性,但主要也是這二種用法。

例 Finally, she found her sister.
　　終於,她找到她妹妹。

例 They succeeded finally.
　　終於,他們成功了。

例 Eric finally knew the truth.
　　最後艾瑞克知道了真相。

例 He finally appeared.
　　最後他出現了。

020

★ Fortunately, S+V...

幸好...

完整句型為Fortunately, S+V.或為 S+V fortunately. 也可為S+ fortunately +V.這裡的fortunately當作副詞,所以要連接兩個句子時,需要and或but兩個連接詞來協助。

例 Fortunately, the doctor saved her life.
幸好,醫生救了她一命。

例 Fortunately, he didn't care about the matter.
幸好,他不在意那件事情。

例 Fortunately, the police caught the thief.
幸好,警察捉到了賊。

例 Fortunately, I passed the test.
幸好,我通過了考試。

★ Frankly speaking, S+V...

坦白說...

完整句型為Frankly speaking, S+V.這裡的frankly speaking也可說成to be frank。

例 Frankly speaking, I like your plan.
坦白說，我喜歡你的計畫。

例 Frankly speaking, I don't like Nick.
坦白說，我不喜歡尼克。

例 Frankly speaking, I don't know the answer.
坦白說，我不知道答案。

例 Frankly speaking, this question is too difficult.
坦白說，這問題實在太難了。

❶ 轉折連結
❷ 表達疑問
❸ 表達情緒
❹ 表達否定
❺ 生活用語

★ Furthermore, S+V...

除此之外...

用法

完整句型為Furthermore, S+V.而 furthermore 等於 besides，皆表示「除了...以外，還有...」的意思，但不可以說 furthermore + N，因為 furthermore 不是介系詞。

另外，這裡的 furthermore 是副詞，若要連接兩個句子，則要加上 and。

例句

例 Furthermore, he has a sports car.
　除此之外，他還有一輛跑車。

例 Furthermore, I have other books.
　除此之外，我還有其他本書。

例 Furthermore, Sam likes delicious food.
　除此之外，山姆也喜歡美食。

例 Furthermore, she knew everything about him.
　除此之外，她知道任何關於他的事情。

★ Honestly, S+V...

說實在地...

完整句型為 Honestly, S+V.或為 S+V, honestly.而
honestly 又可等於 to be honest(常置於句首)。

例 Honestly, he is innocent.

說實在地,他是無辜的。

例 Honestly, I don't blame her.

說實在地,我並不怪她。

例 Honestly, Vincent told the lie.

說實在地,文森說謊。

例 Honestly, we can't believe him.

說實在地,我們無法信任他。

★ However, S+V...

然而；無論如何...

用法

完整句型為 However, S+V. 或為 S+V; however, S+V. 這裡的分號有連接詞的作用，可用來連接兩個句子，例如：I like here; however, I have to leave tomorrow. (我喜歡這裡，然而我明天還是得走。)

例句

例 However, he lost his parents.
然而，他還是失去了他的雙親。

例 However, they got married.
然而，他們還是結婚了。

例 However, I won't give up.
無論如何，我都不會放棄。

例 However, I will always wait for you.
無論如何，我會一直等你。

★ If S+V...

如果...

用法

完整句型為If S1+V1, S2+V2.這裡的if可當作條件句或假設句用,而其詳細的用法就如同even if,因此在這裡就不多加贅述。

例句

📖 If you invite Jack, he will come.
如果你邀請傑克,他會來的。

📖 If it rains tomorrow, I will stay home.
如果明天下雨,我會待在家。

📖 If I were you, I would tell the truth.
如果我是你,我就會說實話。

📖 If she studied hard, she would pass the test.
如果她用功讀書,她就會通過考試。

★ In addition, S+V...

除此之外...

完整句型為 In addition,S+V.這裡的 in addition 也等於 besides 和 furthermore，皆表示"除了...以外，還有"...的意思。另外，in addition 後面若要加名詞，則要加上 to，例如：In addition to English, Jack has to learn Japanese.(除了英語之外，傑克還得學日語。)

例 In addition, they went to many places.
　　除此之外，他們還去了許多地方。

例 In addition, he is a teacher.
　　除此之外，他還是一位老師。

例 In addition, she cleans the house every day.
　　除此之外，她每天都打掃家裡。

例 In addition, I have to finish it before tomorrow.
　　除此之外，我還要在明天之前完成。

★ In fact, S+V...
實際上...

完整句型為 In fact, S+V.也可為 S+V; in fact, S+V.同樣地，這裡的分號當作連接詞，等同於 and 的用法。例如：I like hamburgers; in fact, I like all of the fast food. (我喜歡漢堡，事實上，我喜歡所有的速食。)而 in fact 也可寫成 actually，或是 as a matter of fact，三者用法皆同。

例 In fact, I did it.
　　實際上，這事是我做的。

例 In fact, he is my boyfriend.
　　實際上，他是我男朋友。

例 In fact, the answer is wrong.
　　實際上，這答案是錯的。

例 In fact, I believe her.
　　實際上，我是相信她的。

❶ 轉折連結　❷ 表達疑問　❸ 表達情緒　❹ 表達否定　❺ 生活用語

★ in order to+V...

為了...

完整句型為In order to V(原形), S+V.或為S+V in order to +V(原形).這裡的in order to其實就等於to，所以也可寫成To + V, S+V.或是S+V to + V.

例 In order to succeed, Ben works hard every day.

為了要成功，班每天努力工作。

例 In order to support his family, he has to make more money.

為了養家，他必須賺更多的錢。

例 He studied hard in order to pass the test.

他用功讀書是為了通過考試。

例 She exercises every day in order to lose weight.

她每天運動是為了減肥。

★ in spite of+N,...

儘管...

用法

完整句型為 S+V in spite of+N.或是 In spite of + N, S+V.而 in spite of + N 就等於 despite + N，後頭不可直接加一完整句子，而須加名詞。若要接一完整句子，則須改成 in spite of the fact that + S+V 或是 despite the fact that + S+V。

例句

例 I went to work in spite of my illness.
儘管我生病，我還是去上班。

例 I exercise every day in spite of many things.
儘管有很多事情，我每天還是會運動。

例 In spite of the typhoon, David went out.
儘管有颱風，大衛還是出門去。

例 In spite of the hard task, I have to solve it.
儘管任務很困難，我還是得把它解決。

❶ 轉折連結　❷ 表達疑問　❸ 表達情緒　❹ 表達否定　❺ 生活用語

030

★ No wonder...

難怪...

用法

完整句型為 No wonder S+V.通常對方在表明了一件事情的始末後，就可以用 no wonder 來回應，以表示原來某人或某事現在會有這樣的情況，是因為之前發生過什麼樣的事。

例句

例 No wonder Kate felt so sad.
難怪凱特這麼傷心。

例 No wonder he got the job.
難怪他得到這份工作。

例 No wonder no one stayed home.
難怪沒有人待在家裡。

例 No wonder you were late for school yesterday.
難怪你昨天上課遲到。

★ not only...but also...

不只...而且...

用法

完整句型為 S+ not only + V but also + V.或為 Not only A but also B+V.這裡的 also 有時會省略不寫，但意思不受影響。另外，not only...but also...是為對等連接詞，所以前後所接的詞性須相同。

例句

 Keller not only ate pizza but also drank beer.

凱勒不只吃了披薩，還喝了啤酒。

例 My brother not only plays baseball but also basketball.

我哥哥不只打棒球，而且還打籃球。

例 Not only Leo but also Kevin broke the cups.

不只李奧，而且還有凱文也打破杯子。

例 Not only you but also I am to blame.

不只你，連我都受責備。

★ not...until...

直到...才...

用法

完整句型為S+ V+ not until S+V.雖然中文為"直到...才...",但本句的句型中需要加上not,用否定的語氣來表示這完整的意思。

例句

例 They didn't stop until the teacher came in.
直到老師進來,他們才停止。

例 He didn't feel well until he took some medicine.
直到服了藥後,他才有好一點。

例 She didn't know this secret until Debby told her.
直到黛比告訴她,她才知道這個秘密。

例 I didn't understand this question until I asked Perry.
直到我問了派瑞,我才了解這個問題。

★ Once S+V,...

一旦...

用法

完整句型為 Once S+V, S+V.這裡的 once 當作連接
詞,可連接兩個句子。也可表示為"一次"或是
"曾經"的意思,但詞性就變成副詞,無法連接
兩個句子。

例句

例 Once you eat it, you will like it.
一旦你吃了它之後,你就會喜歡上它。

例 Once you enter the classroom, you have
to follow the rules.
一旦你進了教室,你就得遵守其規則。

例 Once she leaves, she won't come back
again.
她一旦離開之後,就不會再回來。

例 Once Paul decides to do it, he won't
change his mind.
保羅一旦下定決心,他就不會更改心意。

❶ 轉折連結　❷ 表達疑問　❸ 表達情緒　❹ 表達否定　❺ 生活用語

★ Regardless of + N, S+V...

不管/不顧...

完整句型為Regardless of + N, S+V.等於 in spite of和despite，後面皆加名詞。

例 Regardless of the typhoon, they went to the beach.

他們不管颱風，仍舊去了海灘。

例 Regardless of danger, he went there alone.

他不顧危險，依舊獨自前往。

例 Regardless of darkness, she drove the car to look for her daughter.

她不管天色已暗，還是開車去找她女兒。

例 Regardless of fire, the firefighters tried to save the people.

消防隊員不顧大火，仍舊試著搶救人群。

★ S+V ; otherwise...

否則...

用法

完整句型為S+V ; otherwise S+V.這裡的 otherwise 雖然和 or 都可以當作否則的意思，但是 or 可以當作連接詞，可是 otherwise 則是副詞，因此必須有分號來協助，連接兩個句子。

例句

例 Henry should work hard; otherwise he will be fired.

亨利應該認真點工作，否則會被開除。

例 He is not here; otherwise he would agree, too.

他不在這裡，要不然他也會同意的。

例 We need to be quiet; otherwise Miss Laura will be angry.

我們要安靜點，否則蘿拉老師會生氣。

例 You should go home earlier; otherwise your parents will be worried.

你應該早點回家，否則你爸媽會擔心。

❶ 轉折連結　❷ 表達疑問　❸ 表達情緒　❹ 表達否定　❺ 生活用語

★ Since S+V/+N...

自從/既然...

完整句型為 Since S+V, S+V.或者為 Since + N, S+
V.前者的 since 為連接詞,所以後面加上一完整句
子;而後者則為介系詞,因此須接名詞。若是表
示"自從"之意,有時間的意涵在內,主要句子
的動詞就要改成現在完成式。

例 Since you don't like here, why do you
stay?

既然你不喜歡這裡,為何你還留下來?

例 Since he left, I haven't heard from him
for ten years.

自從他離開後,我已經十年沒他的消息。

例 Since last year, my brother hasn't come
home yet.

從去年起至今,我哥哥到現在還沒回來。

例 Since Frank is not here, I will visit him
next time.

既然法蘭克不在這裡,我下次再來拜訪。

★ so...that...

如此...以至於...

用法

完整句型為S+V+ so+形容詞+ that S+V.這裡的 so 不用too,因為這是習慣用法。而這裡的that有表示"以至於"的意思。

例句

📝 I am so hungry that I want to eat more.
我好餓,所以我想再多吃點。

📝 She is so nice that everyone likes her.
她是這麼的好,所以大家都喜歡她。

📝 It is so dark here that I can't see anything.
這裡太暗了,所以我看不到任何東西。

📝 The movie is so great that I want to see it again.
這部電影太好看了,我還想再看一次。

★ Suddenly, S+V...

突然間...

完整句型為 Suddenly, S+V. 或為 S+ suddenly +V.
此處的 suddenly 為副詞，通常置於句首或句中。

例 Suddenly, Sally cried.
突然間，莎莉哭了起來。

例 Suddenly, I heard something strange.
突然間，我聽到奇怪的聲音。

例 He suddenly fell from the chair.
他突然從椅子上倒下來。

例 My computer suddenly stopped working.
我的電腦突然當機了。

★ Thanks to+N,...

幸虧/由於...

用法

完整句型為Thanks to +N, S+V.而 thanks to 也等於 owing to，或是 because of，三者後面皆加上名詞。

例句

例 Thanks to Kevin's help, I could get a job.
幸虧有凱文的協助，我才能找到工作。

例 Thanks to you, I feel better now.
幸虧有你，我現在覺得好多了。

例 Thanks to everyone, we finally finished the work.
由於大家的努力，我們終於完成這項工作。

例 Thanks to the police, we found our car.
由於警察，我們才找到車子。

轉折連結

表達疑問

表達情緒

表達否定

生活用語

040

★ The moment S+V...

當...

完整句型為 The moment S+V, S+V.這裡的 moment 可換成 second 和 instant。而其用法與 when 相同。

例 The moment I went out, I saw a beauty.
當我出門時,我看見了一個美女。

例 The moment she saw the sight, she laughed.
當她看到那畫面時,她笑了。

例 The moment he woke up, he didn't see his wife.
當他起床時,他沒有看到他老婆。

例 The moment we arrived, the bus had gone.
我們到達時,公車已經走了。

★ Unless S+V...

除非...

用法

完整句型為 Unless S+V, S+V. 中文常講 "除非...否則/不然...",但在英文裡,unless 不可和表達 "否則/不然" 的 or/otherwise 放在同一句子裡。只能選其一來使用。

例句

例 Unless you work hard, you will lose this job.

除非你努力工作,否則你會失去這份工作。

例 Unless he tries hard, she won't say yes.

除非他努力嘗試,不然她不會答應的。

例 Unless you tell me the truth, I won't leave.

除非你告訴我事實,不然我不會離開。

例 Unless they finish the task, they can't go home.

除非他們完成這項任務,不然就不能回家。

★ When S+V...

當…

完整句型為When S+V, S+V.這裡的when為連接詞，可用來連接兩個句子，與as soon as的意思及用法相同。

例 When I grow up, I want to be a doctor.
當我長大後，我要當醫生。

例 When you enter the office, please close the door.
當你進入辦公室時，請關門。

例 When you leave, don't forget to turn off the light.
當你離開時，別忘了關燈。

例 When Randy heard the news, he burst into tears.
當藍迪聽到那消息時，他突然大哭。

★ whether...or not

是否...

完整句型為S1+V1 whether S2+V2 or not.句中的 or not可以省略，不影響意思的表達。而這裡的 whether是連接詞，可連接兩個句子。

例 I don't know whether he will come or not.
我不知道他是否會來。

例 I'm not sure whether the meeting will be cancelled or not.
我不確定會議是否會取消掉。

例 He wants to know whether she will finish the work or not.
他想知道是否她能完成這工作。

例 She asked me whether I would join the game or not.
她問我是否我會參加這場比賽。

① 轉折連結

② 表達疑問

③ 表達情緒

④ 表達否定

⑤ 生活用語

044

🎧 track 1-22

★ would rather...

寧願...

完整句型為S+ would rather+V.但通常would rather 後面還會加上than，來表式"寧願...也不要..."之 意。例如：I would rather go out with my sister than stay home with my mom. (我寧願和我妹出 去，也不要和我媽待在家裡。)所以這裡的than有 比較之意。寧願做的事情就緊接在would rather後 面，且要注意的是，would rather + V(原形)， than後面也要加V(原形)，此為對等連接詞。

例 I would rather stay home and watch TV.
我寧願待在家裡看電視。

例 I would rather go out with my mom.
我寧願和我媽出門。

例 I would rather take a bus to work.
我寧願搭公車去上班。

例 I would rather wash dishes than do homework
我寧願洗碗，也不要做功課。

Chapter 2

表達疑問

★ Are you ready to...?

你準備好要...？

完整句型為 Are you ready to+ V(原形)?也可以寫成 Are you ready for + N?

例 Are you ready to go?
你準備好要出發了嗎？

例 Are you ready to do it?
你準備好要做了嗎？

例 Are you ready to join us?
你準備好要加入我們了嗎？

例 Are you ready to face her?
你準備好要面對她了嗎？

★ Are you sure that...?

你確定...?

用法

完整句型為 Are you sure that S+V ?這裡的that可以省略,不會影響句意。因為that後面接了一個完整的句子,所以that才可以省略。

例句

例 Are you sure that Grey will come on time?

你確定葛雷會準時來嗎?

例 Are you sure that she won't make mistakes?

你確定她不會犯錯嗎?

例 Are you sure that no one knows the truth?

你確定沒人知道真相嗎?

例 Are you sure that he is your friend?

你確定他是你朋友嗎?

❶ 轉折連結　❷ 表達疑問　❸ 表達情緒　❹ 表達否定　❺ 生活用語

★ Are you+Ving...?

　你在...嗎？

完整句型為Are you +Ving (現在進行式)?因為are
是be動詞之一，所以其後的動詞要加上ing。

例 Are you doing homework?

　　你在做功課嗎？

例 Are you watching TV?

　　你在看電視嗎？

例 Are you cooking?

　　你在煮飯嗎？

例 Are you calling me?

　　你在叫我嗎？

★ Can you...?

你可以...?

完整句型為 Can you + V (原形)?這裡的can是助動詞,所以後面的動詞要用原形表示。

例 Can you teach me?

你可以教我嗎?

例 Can you do me a favor?

你可以幫我一個忙嗎?

例 Can you give me a ride?

你可以載我一程嗎?

例 Can you show me the way?

你可以告訴我方向嗎?

049

★ Could it be...?

它有可能...?

用法

完整句型為 Could it be +Adj.(形容詞)? 這裡的 it 可指任何事情或某個東西。

例句

例 Could it be hard?

它會很難嗎?

例 Could it be true?

它有可能是真的嗎?

例 Could it be possible?

它是有可能的嗎?

例 Could it be hot there?

那裡會熱嗎?

★ Could you please...?

可以請你...？

用法

完整句型為Could you please+ V (原形)? 加上
please表示更有禮貌的請求。

例 Could you please help me?
可以請你幫我嗎？

例 Could you please stop?
可以請你停下來嗎？

例 Could you please be quiet?
可以請你安靜嗎？

例 Could you please go home now?
可以請你現在回家嗎？

★ Did you+V...?

你有...？

用法

完整句型為Did you +V (原形) ?這裡的助動詞用do的過去式did，表示曾做過某事的意思。有時會和表示過去時間的時間副詞一起用，如：yesterday (昨天)、last night(昨晚)、last month(上個月)……等等。

例句

🔵 Did you go to school yesterday?
你昨天有去上學嗎？

🔵 Did you sleep well last night?
你昨晚有睡好嗎？

🔵 Did you finish your work?
你工作做完了嗎？

🔵 Did you go there last time?
你上次有去那裡嗎？

★ Do I have to...?

我一定要...？

用法

完整句型為Do I have to +V (原形)?通常當別人要求你做某一件你不太願意做的事情時，你就可以用這句話回應。

例句

例 Do I have to eat it?

我一定要吃這玩意嗎？

例 Do I have to do this?

我一定要這麼做嗎？

例 Do I have to go with Danny?

我一定得跟丹尼一起去嗎？

例 Do I have to finish it now?

我一定現在就要完成嗎？

★ Do you have...?

你有...？

用法

完整句型為 Do you have + N ?當你需要某個東西時，就可以用此句型詢問他人。

例句

例 Do you have time?

你有空嗎？

例 Do you have a pen?

你有筆嗎？

例 Do you have this book?

你有這本書嗎？

例 Do you have one hundred dollars?

你有一百塊嗎？

★ Do you know how to...?

你知道該如何...？

用法

完整句型為 Do you know how to +V (原形)? 當你不曉得該如何處理某事情時，就可用這句型詢問他人，請對方示範一次給你看。

例句

🔹 Do you know how to cook?

你知道該怎麼煮飯嗎？

🔹 Do you know how to go there?

你知道該怎麼去那裡嗎？

🔹 Do you know how to open the box?

你知道該怎麼打開這盒子嗎？

🔹 Do you know how to operate the machine?

你知道該如何操作這台機器嗎？

❶ 轉折連結

❷ 表達疑問

❸ 表達情緒

❹ 表達否定

❺ 生活用語

★ Do you think...?

你覺得...？

完整句型為 Do you think that S+V ?這裡的 that 可以省略，因為 that 後面接一完整句子。

例 Do you think we will win?

你覺得我們會贏嗎？

例 Do you think she will show up?

你覺得她會出現嗎？

例 Do you think that he can do it?

你覺得他能做這件事嗎？

例 Do you think that it is a good idea?

你覺得這是好主意嗎？

★ Do you understand...?

你了解...？

用
法

完整句型為 Do you understand + N?或是 Do you
understand what S+V?或是 Do you understand how
to +V (原形)?

例
句

🔘 Do you understand this question?

你了解這問題嗎？

🔘 Do you understand Japanese?

你懂日文嗎？

🔘 Do you understand how to answer the
question?

你懂該如何回答這問題嗎？

🔘 Do you understand what I am talking
about?

你了解我所說的嗎？

057 🎧track 2-7

★ Do you want to...?

你想要...？

完整句型為 Do you want to +V (原形)？當你問別人想不想做某事時，就可以用此句型來問。

例 Do you want to leave now?

你想現在離開嗎？

例 Do you want to have some coffee?

你想喝咖啡嗎？

例 Do you want to see a movie?

你想看電影嗎？

例 Do you want to eat in a restaurant?

你想去餐廳吃飯嗎？

★ Does he still...?

他仍然...?

用法

完整句型為Does he still +V (原形)？這裡的he
可以換成其他第三人稱，例如：she或是人名。當
然也可換成Do you/we/they still...?

例句

例 Does he still like her?
他還喜歡她嗎？

例 Does he still live here?
他仍然住在這裡嗎？

例 Does he still work in this company?
他仍然在這間公司上班嗎？

例 Does he still play basketball every day?
他仍然每天打籃球嗎？

★ Have you ever...?

你曾經...?

用法

完整句型為 Have you ever+ Vpp (分詞) ?這裡的 have 作為助動詞用,但後面的動詞型態須改成分詞,也就是 have+Vpp 現在完成式。

例句

📻 Have you ever been there?
你去過那裡嗎?

📻 Have you ever seen this person?
你曾經見過這個人嗎?

📻 Have you ever tasted the food?
你嚐過這種食物嗎?

📻 Have you ever been to Japan?
你曾去過日本嗎?

★ How about+Ving...?

不然...?

用法

完整句型為 How about + Ving?由於about是介系詞,所以後面的動詞須改成 Ving。而這裡的how可以改成 what。

例句

🔹 How about going out now?

不然現在出去好了?

🔹 How about seeing a movie tonight?

不然今晚來看電影好了?

🔹 How about staying home and watching TV?

不然待在家裡看電視好了?

🔹 How about having dinner with me this weekend?

不然這周末和我一起吃晚餐如何?

061

🎧track 2-9

★ How could you...?

你怎麼可以... ?

完整句型為 How could you + V(原形)？could 為助動詞，所以後面的動詞要用原形。而 you 可改成其他主詞，例如：he/she/we/they/人名。

例 How could you give up?

你怎麼可以放棄呢？

例 How could you do this to me?

你怎麼可以對我做出這種事呢？

例 How could you cheat on exams?

你怎麼可以作弊呢？

例 How could you abandon your family?

你怎麼可以拋棄你的家人呢？

★ How dare...?

你怎敢...?

用法

完整句型為 How dare S+V(原形)? 這裡的 dare 為助動詞，因此其後的動詞為原形動詞。

例句

例 How dare he just grab her hand?
他怎敢就這樣抓住她的手？

例 How dare they scream in public?
他們怎敢在大眾面前尖叫？

例 How dare you ask him such a question?
你怎敢問他這樣的問題？

例 How dare you do this without my permission?
你怎敢未經我允許就這麼做？

063

★ How do you feel...?

你感覺如何...？

完整句型為 How do you feel about+ N/ Ving ?因為 about 為介系詞，所以後面可加名詞或是 Ving。

例 How do you feel about this matter?
你對這件事覺得如何？

例 How do you feel about the test?
你對這考試有何看法？

例 How do you feel about his leaving?
對於他的離去你有何看法？

例 How do you feel about going out with Ted?
你對於和泰德一起出去，有什麼感覺？

★ How do you know that...?

你怎麼知道...?

用法

完整句型為 How do you know that S+V? 這裡的 that 可省略不寫，若後面接一個完整句子。

例句

例 How do you know that he loves you?
你怎麼知道他愛你?

例 How do you know that she is serious?
你怎麼知道她是當真的?

例 How do you know she works here?
你怎麼知道她在這裡工作?

例 How do you know this is my dad's letter?
你怎麼知道這是我爸的信?

★ How far is it from...?

從...有多遠...？

 用法

完整句型為How far is it from +N to +N ?這裡的名詞皆為地點，另外，這裡的it不可用其他字替代，這是固定用法。而這裡的it則是指距離。

 例句

例 How far is it from here to there?
從這裡到那裡有多遠？

例 How far is it from my home to your home?
從我家到你家有多遠？

例 How far is it from this park to that school?
從這公園到那學校有多遠？

例 How far is it from this bus stop to the hospital?
從這公車站到那間醫院有多遠？

★ How long does it take...?

...要花多久的時間？

用法

完整句型為 How long does it take to + V(原形)? 或是 How long does it take from +N to +N ?這裡的 how long 不是指距離，而是指所花的時間，也就是 it。且這裡的 it 不可用其他字替代，這是固定用法。

例句

例 How long does it take to go to school every day?

你每天上學要花多久的時間？

例 How long does it take to finish your homework?

你要花多久的時間完成功課？

例 How long does it take to take a shower?

你洗澡要花多久的時間？

例 How long does it take to drive from here to your home?

從這裡開車到你家要花多久的時間？

英語句型 這樣學才會快

★ How long have you...?

你已經...多久了?

用法

完整句型為How long have you +Vpp(分詞)?因為
此句表示"從事某事的一段時間",所以這裡的
動詞型態為現在完成式,即從過去到現在為止的
這段時間。若主詞改成第三人稱,動詞形式則為
has + Vpp。

例句

📙 How long have you read the book?
你這本書已經讀多久了?

📙 How long have you lived here?
你住在這裡已經多久了?

📙 How long have you learned English?
你學英文學多久了?

📙 How long have you worked in this
company?
你在這間公司工作多久了?

★ How many...?

有多少...？

完整句型為 How many ＋複數可數 N＋助動詞+S＋
V(原形)?或為 How many ＋複數可數 N ＋ be 動詞？
而這裡的助動詞最常使用的是 do 和 does，有時候
也可用 can。因為 many 表示許多，所以後面要加
可數名詞的複數形，例如：how many pens/apples/
dollars 等等。

例 How many people are there?

那裡有多少人？

例 How many dollars do you have?

你有多少錢？

例 How many books do you read every day?

你每天讀多少本書？

例 How many toys does your brother have?

你弟弟有多少玩具？

★ How many times have you...?

你多少次...?

用法

完整句型為How many times have you+ Vpp(分詞)?這裡的句型是要表達"從過去某段時間到現在"所做之事的次數,因此動詞須改成現在完成式。

例句

例 How many times have you called me?
你打給我多少次了?

例 How many times have you lied to me?
你騙我多少次了?

例 How many times have you been to Hong Kong?
你到香港多少次了?

例 How many times have you been late for school?
你上學遲到多少次了?

★ How much...?

...多少？

用法

完整句型為 How much +單數不可數名詞+助動詞+ S+V(原形)?這裡的單數不可數名詞可為mo-ney/water等，而常用的助動詞為do或does。

例句

📖 How much money do you have?
你有多少錢？

📖 How much money does it cost?
這東西多少錢？

📖 How much water is there in the glass?
這杯子裡有多少水？

📖 How much money do you earn in a month?
你一個月賺多少錢？

❶ 轉折連結

❷ 表達疑問

❸ 表達情緒

❹ 表達否定

❺ 生活用語

071

track 2-14

★ Is it possible to+V...?

有可能... ？

完整句型為Is it possible to +V(原形)?若要針對某個對象而言，則可寫成Is it possible for +S + to +V(原形)。這裡的is it為固定用法，不可改變。

例 Is it possible for Ryan to win the game?
萊恩有可能贏得這比賽嗎？

例 Is it possible for Ian to tell me the secret?
伊恩有可能告訴我秘密嗎？

例 Is it possible to live without fear?
人有可能過著沒有恐懼的生活嗎？

例 Is it possible for me to pass the exam in three months?
我有可能在三個月內通過考試嗎？

★ Is that...?

那是... ?

用法

完整句型為 Is that+ N ?這裡的名詞為單數名詞，因為前有 is。而 that 可換成 this。若為複數名詞，則用 Are those/these 來表示，例如：Are these your pens?(這些是你的筆嗎？)

例句

例 Is that your book?

那是你的書嗎？

例 Is that your cell phone?

那是你的手機嗎？

例 Is that her name?

那是她的名字嗎？

例 Is that his computer?

那是他的電腦嗎？

073　　　　　　　　　🎧 track 2-15

★ Is there anything wrong with...?

...有什麼問題嗎？

 用法

完整句型為 Is there anything wrong with +N？某件事情或東西有問題，介系詞習慣上會用 with。

 例句

例 Is there anything wrong with my face?
我的臉有問題嗎？

例 Is there anything wrong with her leg?
她的腿有什麼問題嗎？

例 Is there anything wrong with this matter?
這件事情有什麼問題嗎？

例 Is there anything wrong with this book?
這本書有什麼問題嗎？

★ May I...?

> 我可以...?

完整句型為May I +V (原形)?這裡的may為助動詞,所以其後的動詞須是原形動詞。

例 May I help you, sir?
先生,需要我幫忙嗎?

例 May I go home now?
我現在可以回家了嗎?

例 May I watch TV?
我可以看電視嗎?

例 May I buy this cell phone?
我可以買這支手機嗎?

★ Should we...?

我們應該... ?

 用法

完整句型為Should we + V(原形)?這裡的should
為助動詞,因此這裡的動詞須為原形動詞。另
外,should在這裡的意思是"應該",所以其語
氣較為強勢點,帶有些許命令或指示的意味。這
裡的we也可換成其他主詞。

 例句

例 Should we leave?

我們該走了吧?

例 Should we stop now?

我們現在應該停止吧?

例 Should we let him go?

我們應該放他走嗎?

例 Should we get started?

我們應該動工了吧?

★ What do you mean that...?

你是指什麼意思？

完整句型為What do you mean that S+V ?此句中that後面的動詞時態可為現在式或過去式，端看使用者所要表達的意思為何。

例 What do you mean that you can't do it?
你說你無法做這件事是什麼意思？

例 What do you mean that you want to quit?
你說你想辭職這是什麼意思？

例 What do you mean that he stole your letter?
你說他偷走你的信是什麼意思？

例 What do you mean that she cheated on you?
你說她對你不忠是什麼意思？

① 轉折連結 ② 表達疑問 ③ 表達情緒 ④ 表達否定 ⑤ 生活用語

★ What do you say to + Ving...?

你覺得不然...？

用法

完整句型為 What do you say to +Ving +N ？這裡
要特別注意的是 to 後面的動詞要加 ing，是固定用
法，因為此句型是從 How about + Ving 演變而來。

例句

例 What do you say to having some coffee now?

你覺得不然現在來喝咖啡如何？

例 What do you say to going to a movie tonight?

你覺得不然今晚去看電影如何？

例 What do you say to coming to my home tomorrow?

你覺得不然明天來我家如何？

例 What do you say to having lunch with me at noon?

你覺得不然中午和我吃飯如何？

★ What do you think...?

你覺得...如何？

用法

完整句型為 What do you think of + N ?或為 What do you think (that) S+V ?

例句

例 What do you think of my new glasses?
你覺得我的新眼鏡看起來如何？

例 What do you think of my performance?
你覺得我的表演如何？

例 What do you think let's get started now?
你覺得我們現在開始動工如何？

例 What do you think she quit her job for?
你對於她辭掉她的工作有何看法？

★ What if...?

假使/萬一...？

完整句型為What if +S + Vpt(過去式)?此句型是假設的語氣，原為What (will/ would happen) if +S+V?的省略。須注意的是，此句中的動詞須為過去式，因此句型是假設語氣。

📝 What if he forgot?
萬一他忘了呢？

📝 What if we did it privately?
假使我們私下進行呢？

📝 What if I left for Japan tomorrow?
假使我明天就去日本呢？

📝 What if they told her the truth?
萬一他們告訴她事實呢？

★ What is/are+N...?

...是什麼？

用法

完整句型為What is/are +N?這裡的名詞為可數名詞，若是單數名詞，就用is，複數名詞則用are。

例句

例 What is this?

這是什麼？

例 What is it?

它是什麼東西？

例 What are these?

這些是什麼東西？

例 What are those colors?

那些顏色是什麼？

❶ 轉折連結

❷ 表達疑問

❸ 表達情緒

❹ 表達否定

❺ 生活用語

081

★ What should we do to...?

我們該怎麼做來...？

完整句型為 What should we do to + V(原形)?當某件事情的結果不是所預期時，可能很糟或是屬於可補救時，就可以用上此句型。

例 What should we do to make it right?
我們該怎麼做才是對的？

例 What should we do to make her happy?
我們該怎麼做才能讓她開心？

例 What should we do to let Benson leave here?
我們該怎麼做才能讓班森離開這裡？

例 What should we do to escape from this place?
我們該怎麼做才能逃離這地方？

★ What time do you...?

你何時...？

完整句型為What time do you +V(原形)?主詞you 可改成其他人稱，但若為第三人稱，如：he/she/ 人名，do就得改成does。

例 What time do you get up?

你幾點起床？

例 What time do you go to work?

你幾點上班？

例 What time do you go home?

你幾點回家？

例 What time do you go to bed?

你幾點睡覺？

轉折連結

② 表達疑問

③ 表達情緒

④ 表達否定

⑤ 生活用語

083 track 2-20

★ What would you like ...?

你想要什麼？

用法

完整句型為What would you like to +V (原形)?
此句型所表達之意等於What do you want to +V (原形)?

例句

例 What would you like to eat?
你想吃什麼？

例 What would you like to write?
你想寫些什麼？

例 What would you like to do now?
你現在想做什麼？

例 What would you like to say to her?
你想對她說什麼？

🎧 track 2-20

★ What would you say if...?

你覺得如果...？

用法

完整句型為What would you say if S+V?這裡的動詞則是用過去式。

例句

📖 What would you say if I accepted Mark?
如果我接受了馬克，你覺得如何？

📖 What would you say if I kissed you?
如果我吻了你，你覺得如何？

📖 What would you say if I gave up?
如果我放棄了，你有什麼想法？

📖 What would you say if I insisted on this plan?
如果我堅持這項計畫，你有什麼看法？

★ When did you...?

你何時...?

用法

完整句型為When did you +V(原形)?這裡的you
可改成he/she/they/we。

例句

例 When did you quit?

你何時離職?

例 When did you leave home?

你何時離開家裡?

例 When did you get up this morning?

你今早幾點起床?

例 When did you send the letter?

你何時寄出這封信?

★ Where do you...?

你在哪裡...？

完整句型為Where do you + V(原形)?若想問之
事為過去式，則將do改為did。

例 Where do you work?
　 你在哪裡工作？

例 Where do you live?
　 你住在哪裡？

例 Where did you go last night?
　 你昨晚去哪裡？

例 Where did you have dinner yesterday?
　 你昨天去哪裡吃晚餐？

087 track 2-22

★ Which+N do you...?

哪一個你...？

用法

完整句型為Which +N do you +V (原形)?這裡的
which為形容詞，後面接單數名詞。

例句

例 Which one do you like?

你喜歡哪一個？

例 Which book do you want?

你想要哪一本書？

例 Which house do you live in?

你住在哪一間房子？

例 Which movie do you like the most?

你最喜歡哪一部電影？

★ Who knows...?

> 誰知道...？

用法

完整句型為 Who knows + N ? 或為 Who knows+ how to + V(原形)+ N ? 也可為 Who knows+ what to + V(原形)? 這裡的 know 在現在式中要加 s。 who 在英文裡是當作第三人稱，因為不知道是 "誰"，所以用第三人稱表示。

例句

例 Who knows them?
誰認識他們？

例 Who knows the news?
誰知道這消息？

例 Who knows how to do it?
誰知道該怎麼做這東西？

例 Who knows what to do?
誰知道該怎麼做？

★ Who said...?

誰說...？

用法

> 完整句型為 Who said S+V？這裡的 say 我們用過
> 去式 said，因為人家說過了，所以用過去式表示。

例句

例 Who said I lie?

誰說我說謊？

例 Who said I like him?

誰說我喜歡他？

例 Who said she is my friend?

誰說她是我朋友？

例 Who said I can't do it?

誰說我沒辦法做這事？

★ Who wants...?

誰想要...?

用法

完整句型為 Who wants +N? 或者是 Who wants to + V(原形)?由於 who "誰" 不確定主詞為第一、二還是第三人稱,因此在英文裡,統一視為第三人稱,所以 want 要加 s。

例句

例 Who wants it?

誰想要這東西?

例 Who wants the book?

誰想要這本書?

例 Who wants to go out?

有誰想出去?

例 Who wants to take a break?

有誰想休息一下?

091

🎧 track 2-24

★ Whose+N...? ...

是誰的...？

用法

> 完整句型為Whose + N+ is/are + 代名詞?由於whose意思為"誰的"，因此主詞不知道是誰，不能寫you/I/he/she/they……等等。句型中的代名詞常為these/ those/ this/that等。

例句

例 Whose books are these?

這些書是誰的？

例 Whose clothes are those?

那些衣服是誰的？

例 Whose pen is this?

這支筆是誰的？

例 Whose house is that?

那棟房子是誰的？

★ Why do you...?

> 為什麼你...？

用法

完整句型為 Why do you+ V(原形)?當你對他人所做之事感到疑惑時，就可以用此句型問對方。當然也可改成 Why doeshs/she/人名...?等用第三人稱表示。

例句

例 Why do you love her?
你為什麼愛她？

例 Why did you quit?
你為什麼辭職？

例 Why did you tell a lie?
你為什麼說謊？

例 Why did you leave without saying goodbye?
你為什麼不告而別？

右側直書：
① 轉折連結
② 表達疑問
③ 表達情緒
④ 表達否定
⑤ 生活用語

093

★ Why don't you...?

你為何不...？

用法

完整句型為 Why don't you + V(原形)? 當你想提供對方一個解決的方法時，就可以用此句型回應。若主詞為第三人稱時，則可改成 Why doesn't he/she/人名...?

例句

例 Why don't you stay here?
你為何不待在這裡？

例 Why don't you leave tomorrow?
你為什麼不明天才走？

例 Why don't you do homework?
你為什麼不寫功課？

例 Why don't you talk to me?
你為什麼不和我說話？

★ Why should I...?

為何我該...？

 用法

完整句型為Why should I +V (原形)?當對方要求或指示你去做某件事情時，而你不太願意，或覺得為何是我要去做時，就可以用此句型回應。

 例句

例 Why should I listen to you?
為什麼我就要聽你的？

例 Why should I do it right now?
為何我現在就該做這事？

例 Why should I say yes to her?
為何我就要答應她？

例 Why should I go out with him?
為什麼我就要和他出去？

★ Would you like to...?

你想要...？

完整句型為Would you like to +V(原形)?此句型的用法及意思就等於Do you want to +V?只是用 would like 表示比較委婉或有禮貌點。

例 Would you like to have some tea?
你想喝茶嗎？

例 Would you like to eat ice cream?
你想吃冰淇淋嗎？

例 Would you like to join the game?
你想參加比賽嗎？

例 Would you like to go out with me?
你想和我出去嗎？

★ Would you mind...?

你介意... ？

完整句型為 Would you mind+Ving? 或是 Would you mind if S+V ? 這裡的 mind 當作 "介意或在意" 時，其後面的動詞要改成 Ving。

例句

例 Would you mind closing the door?
可以請你把門帶上嗎？

例 Would you mind turning on the lights?
可以請你開燈嗎？

例 Would you mind if I smoke?
你介意我抽菸嗎？

例 Would you mind if I stay here?
你介意我待在這裡嗎？

097

★ Would you please...?

可以請你...?

完整句型為Would you please + V(原形)?此句是請求協助的語氣，且是蠻有禮貌的用法。類似 Could you please...?的用法。

例 Would you please open the window?
　　可以請你打開窗戶嗎？

例 Would you please come here?
　　你可以過來這裡一下嗎？

例 Would you please lend me a pen?
　　可以請你借我一支筆嗎？

例 Would you please cooperate with us?
　　可以請你配合我們一下嗎？

Chapter 3

表達情緒

098 track 3-1

★ A is fed up with +N...

A 受夠了...

用法

完整句型為A+ be V(Be動詞) +fed up with+N.此
句也可說A+ can't stand/tolerate/bear+ N.或是A is
tired of +N.此句中的N可為人或事、物。

例
句

例 I am fed up with you.

我受夠你了。

例 I am fed up with the noise.

我受夠了那噪音。

例 She is fed up with her mom.

她受夠了她母親。

例 Ted is fed up with the work.

泰德受夠了那份工作。

★ A is proud of...

A 對...為傲(榮)

用法

完整句型為A is proud of+ N.此句的N可為人或事。而句中的is可隨主詞的更換而改變。

例句

例 I am proud of you.
我以你為傲。

例 My dad is proud of me.
我爸以我為榮。

例 I am proud of my country.
我以我的國家為榮。

例 She is proud of her son.
她以她的兒子為傲。

❶ ❷ ❾

❶ 轉折連結

❷ 表達疑問

❸ 表達情緒

❹ 表達否定

❺ 生活用語

★ A is such a...

A 是如此的...

完整句型為A is such a +N. 此句所表達之意可
為正面的讚美或負面的批評，視說話者欲表達的
意思而定。

例
句

例 Tracy is such a beautiful girl.

崔西真是一位可人兒。

例 You are such a fool.

你真是個笨蛋。

例 That is such a great job.

那真是一份棒極的工作。

例 It is such a nice day.

今天天氣真是好。

★ A is worried that/ about+N...

A 擔心...

用法

> 完整句型為A+ be動詞 worried that S+V.或是 A + be動詞 worried about+ N.前者是子句的概念，可把句意說得更詳細清楚。而後者則直接表明所擔心之人事物。

例句

例 I am very worried about you.
我很擔心你。

例 My mom is always worried about my safety.
我媽總是擔心我的安全。

例 He was worried that he would lose you.
他擔心他會失去你。

例 We are worried that you will be late.
我們擔心你會遲到。

★ A is worth...

A 值得...

完整句型為 A is worth +Ving /N.這裡的動詞一定
要加 ing，為特定用法。

🔘 It is worth a try.

這值得一試。

🔘 The house is worth a visit.

這房子值得一覽。

🔘 The book is worth reading.

這本書值得一讀。

🔘 The movie is not worth seeing.

這部片不值得一看。

★ be afraid of...

恐怕...

用法

完整句型為S+ be V+ afraid of+ N.也可寫成 S+ be V+ afraid to+ V(原形動詞)，或是A+ be V+ afraid that S+V.

例句

例 I am afraid of the test.
我擔心這場考試。

例 Kate is afraid of snakes.
凱特怕蛇。

例 My brother is afraid of my dad.
我弟怕我爸。

例 I am not afraid of you.
我才不怕你。

❶轉折連結
❷表達疑問
❸表達情緒
❹表達否定
❺生活用語

★ be angry at...

對...生氣

用法

完整句型為S+ be V+ angry at+ N.這裡須注意的是,對誰生氣,介系詞是用at。這裡的angry也可改成mad(生氣的、火大的)。

例句

例 Don't be angry at me.
不要對我生氣。

例 I am angry at you.
我對你感到生氣。

例 My dad was angry at my sister.
我爸對我姐覺得很生氣。

例 Sally was not angry at Sam.
莎莉沒有對山姆生氣。

★ be curious about...

對...好奇

完整句型為S+ be V+ curious about+ N.也可寫成
A+ be V+ curious that S+V.

🔹 He is curious about people.

他對人感到好奇。

🔹 I am curious about the new student.

我對那位新生感到好奇。

🔹 The little boy is curious about everything.

那個小男孩對每件事都感到好奇。

🔹 My boss is curious about the plan.

我的老闆對這計畫感到好奇。

英語
句型

這樣學
才會快

★ be glad to...

對...感到高興

用法

> 完整句型為S+ be V+ glad to + V(原形動詞).也
> 可寫成A + be V+ glad that S+V.此句中的glad也
> 可用happy替換。

例句

例 I am glad to meet you.

我很高興見到你。

例 I am glad to hear the news.

我很高興聽到那消息。

例 I am glad to do it for you.

我很高興為你做這事。

例 I am glad to have dinner with you.

我很高興與你共進晚餐。

① ③ ⑦

★ have no choice but to...

不得不...

用法

完整句型為 S+ have/has/had no choice but to + V(原形動詞).此句也可表示為 S+ have/has/had to +V(原形動詞)。

例句

🔵 I have no choice but to leave now.
我現在不得不離開。

🔵 We have no choice but to stay here.
我們沒有選擇，只能待在這裡。

🔵 She had no choice but to marry him.
她沒有選擇，只好嫁給他。

🔵 He had no choice but to take the job.
他沒有選擇，只得接下那份工作。

① 轉折連結

② 表達疑問

③ 表達情緒

④ 表達否定

⑤ 生活用語

★ I agree...

我同意、贊成...

 用法

完整句型為 I agree that S+V. 句中的 that 可以省略，因為後面有一完整句子(主詞加動詞)。也可寫成 I agree with+ N. 表示贊成某人的意思。

 例句

📖 I agree with your plan.
我贊成你的計畫。

📖 He didn't agree with my opinion.
他不贊成我的意見。

📖 I agreed that he was the winner.
我同意他是冠軍。

📖 I agree that you join the game.
我贊成你參賽。

★ I feel...

我覺得...

用法

完整句型為I feel that S+V.也可有I feel +Adj.(形容詞)這兩種常見用法。

 例句

例 I feel so cold.
我覺得好冷。

例 I feel sad.
我覺得很難過。

例 I felt that she got sick.
我感覺她好像生病了。

例 I felt that something would happen.
我感覺好像有事會發生。

① 轉折連結

② 表達疑問

③ 表達情緒

④ 表達否定

⑤ 生活用語

★ I find it difficult to...

我認為...是有困難的

完整句型為 I find it difficult to + V(原形動詞).
此句也可寫成 Something is difficult for me to +
V (原形動詞).而 difficult 可以改成 hard。

例 I find it difficult to finish the work.
我認為要完成這工作是有困難的。

例 I find it difficult to solve the problem.
我覺得要解決這問題是困難的。

例 I find it difficult to talk with Frank.
我覺得和法蘭克講話是困難的一件事。

例 I find it difficult to succeed.
我覺得成功是困難的。

★ I hate...

我討厭...

完整句型為 I hate+N.或為 I hate to+ V(原形動詞)/ Ving.這裡的to，後面動詞可為to+ V原，或是Ving。

例 I hate you.
　我討厭你。

例 I hate the smell.
　我討厭那個味道。

例 I hate to do it.
　我討厭做這件事。

例 I hate to go out with him.
　我討厭和他出去。

★ I have a good time...

...玩得愉快

用法

完整句型為 I have a good time+ Ving/ with+人.
此句也等於 I have fun + Ving/ with+人。

例句

 I had a good time with Kelly.
我和凱莉處得很愉快。

 I had a good time with David's family.
我和大衛的家人相處得很愉快。

 I had a good time playing basketball yesterday.
我昨天打籃球打得很開心。

 I had a good time going out with Molly last weekend.
上周末，我和茉莉出去，玩得很開心。

★ I have a problem...

我對...有問題

完整句型為I have a problem with+ N.以及I have a problem (in)+ Ving.後者的in通常會省略,所以只會看到have a problem+ Ving的部分。

例 I have a problem with the work.
我對這工作有問題。

例 I have a problem with sleep.
我睡眠有問題。

例 I have a problem finishing the plan.
我對完成這計畫有問題。

例 I have a problem doing my homework.
我對我的功課有問題。

❶ 轉折連結

❷ 表達疑問

❸ 表達情緒

❹ 表達否定

❺ 生活用語

★ I look forward to...

我期待...

用法

完整句型為I look forward to + Ving/ N.也可寫成I expect that S+V.或是I anticipate+ Ving/N.皆表示期待之意。這裡動詞為Ving的部分是特定用法，須注意。

例句

例 I look forward to your good news.
我期待你的好消息。

例 I look forward to his coming.
我期待他的到來。

例 I look forward to seeing that movie.
我期待看那部電影。

例 I look forward to having lunch with Dora.
我期待和朵拉共進晚餐。

★ I object...

我反對...

用法

完整句型為 I object to+N/Ving. 或為 I object that S+V. 這裡的 object to+Ving 是特定用法，須注意。

例句

例 I objected to the plan.
我反對這計畫。

例 I objected to your idea.
我反對你的意見。

例 I objected that he joined our team.
我反對他加入我們這一組。

例 I objected that she took the job.
我反對她接下這份工作。

❶ 轉折連結

❷ 表達疑問

❸ 表達情緒

❹ 表達否定

❺ 生活用語

★ I prefer...

我偏好...

用法

完整句型為I prefer that S+V.或是I prefer A to B./I prefer +N./ I prefer Ving./ I prefer to+V(原形動詞)。

例句

例 I prefer this white T-shirt.
我比較喜歡這件白色T恤。

例 I prefer coffee to tea.
我喜歡咖啡勝過於茶。

例 I prefer to watch TV.
我比較喜歡看電視。

例 I prefer staying at home.
我比較喜歡待在家。

★ I promise I will...

我保證我會...

用法

完整句型為 I promise I will +V(原形動詞).若為否定句，則寫為 I promise I won't/ will never +V (原形動詞)。

例句

例 I promise I will finish the work.
我保證我會完成這工作。

例 I promise I will make it.
我保證我會做到。

例 I promise I won't leave you.
我保證我不會離開你。

例 I promise I won't cheat on you.
我保證我不會背棄你。

❶ 轉折連結

❷ 表達疑問

❸ 表達情緒

❹ 表達否定

❺ 生活用語

★ I'm happy to...

我很高興...

用法

完整句型為I'm happy to+ V(原形動詞).

例句

例 I'm happy to come here.
我很高興來到這裡。

例 I'm happy to have dinner with you.
我很高興與你共進晚餐。

例 I'm happy to visit your home.
我很高興來拜訪你家。

例 I'm happy to be your friend.
我很高興能當你的朋友。

★ I'm interested in...

我對...有興趣

用法

完整句型為I'm interested in +N/ Ving.或為I'm interested to +V(原形動詞)。

例句

🔘 I'm interested in English.
我對英文有興趣。

🔘 I'm interested in your job.
我對你的工作感到興趣。

🔘 I'm interested in cooking.
我對烹飪有興趣。

🔘 I'm interested in playing basketball.
我對打籃球有興趣。

❶ 轉折連結

❷ 表達疑問

❸ 表達情緒

❹ 表達否定

❺ 生活用語

★ I'm sorry to+V/that...

我很抱歉...

用法

完整句型為I'm sorry to+ V(原形動詞).或是I'm sorry that S+V.

例句

例 I'm sorry to hurt you.
我很抱歉傷了你。

例 I'm sorry to hear the news.
我很遺憾聽到這消息。

例 I'm sorry that I can't stay here.
我很抱歉我無法待在此地。

例 I'm sorry that I can't join the game.
我很抱歉我無法參加這比賽。

★ I'm thankful for+N...

我很感激...

用法

> 完整句型為I'm thankful for+ N(事)/Ving。這裡若
> 要加動詞，要記得加上Ving等。

例句

🔲 I'm thankful for your comfort.
我很感謝你的安慰。

🔲 I'm thankful for their support.
我很感謝他們的支持。

🔲 I was thankful for his help.
我很感激他的幫忙。

🔲 I was thankful for her advice.
我很感謝她的建議。

❶ 轉折連結

❷ 表達疑問

❸ 表達情緒

❹ 表達否定

❺ 生活用語

★ It is much (more) + Adj....

...比較...的多了

用法

完整句型為It is much+ 比較級Adj.(形容詞).而這裡的it則是可指任何事情、方式或是天氣等不具生命的事物,且it不可改成人。另外,加上much則是有強調的語氣。

例句

例 It is much better.
這樣子好多了。

例 It is much cooler today.
今天天氣涼多了。

例 It is much easier.
這樣子簡單多了。

例 It is much more convenient this way.
這樣方便多了。

★ It is+Adj.+to...

...是...

用法

完整句型為 It is +Adj. + to V(原形動詞).這裡的
It 不可改成其他主詞，此為特定用法。用來代指
to+V(動詞)後面所指之事。

例句

例 It is great to work here.
在這裡上班很棒。

例 It is cold to walk outside.
在外面走路很冷。

例 It is dangerous to drive fast.
急速駕駛很危險。

例 It is safe to stay here.
待在此很安全。

★ It tastes like...

它嚐起來像...

完整句型為 It tastes like + N. 也可寫成 It tastes + Adj. 前者加上 like，表示有 "像" 的意思，較為具體的形容詞。

例 It tastes like chicken.
它嚐起來像雞肉

例 It tastes like pudding.
它嚐起來像布丁。

例 It tastes delicious.
這嚐起來太美味了。

例 It tastes bitter.
這嚐起來有苦味。

★ It's a pity...

可惜...

用法

完整句型為It's a pity that S+V.

例句

例 It's a pity that you lost the game.
你輸了那比賽真可惜。

例 It's a pity that she didn't come.
她沒來真可惜。

例 It's a pity that he went out.
可惜他出門去了。

例 It's a pity that Larry was late.
可惜賴瑞遲到。

❶ 轉折連結

❷ 表達疑問

❸ 表達情緒

❹ 表達否定

❺ 生活用語

★ It's good to...

...很好(棒)

用法

完整句型為It's good to + V(原形動詞),也可寫成
It's good for A to+V(原形動詞)。一句有加上人
的名稱,另一句則無,視表達者意思而定。

例
句

例 It's good to see you.
看到你真好。

例 It's good to be with you.
跟你在一起真好。

例 It's good to hear the news.
聽到這消息真好。

例 It's good to have a good friend.
有好朋友真好。

★ It's important to...

...是重要的

 用法

> 完整句型為It's important to +V (原形動詞).

 例句

例 It's important to do homework.
做功課是重要的。

例 It's important to finish the work.
完成這工作是很重要的。

例 It's important to check again.
再檢查一次是很重要的。

例 It's important to have breakfast every day.
每天要吃早餐是很重要的。

❶ 轉折連結

❷ 表達疑問

❸ 表達情緒

❹ 表達否定

❺ 生活用語

★ It's impossible to...

...是不可能的

用法

完整句型為It's impossible to +V (原形動詞).

例句

🔵 It's impossible to live with him.
我是不可能和他住在一起的。

🔵 It's impossible to go out with her.
我是不可能和她出去的。

🔵 It's impossible to achieve the goal.
要達成那目標是不可能的。

🔵 It's impossible to solve the difficult problem.
要解決那困難的問題是不可能的。

★ It's kind of A to+V...

...真好...

用法

完整句型為It's kind of A to +V (原形動詞)。這裡的A是受詞的型態，而非主詞，例如：him, her, you, them以及人名。

例句

例 It's kind of you to help me a lot.
你人真好，幫了我許多忙。

例 It's kind of you to lend me money.
你人真好，借錢給我。

例 It's kind of him to give me the book.
他人真好，給我那本書。

例 It's kind of her to teach me English.
她人真好，教我英文。

❶ 轉折連結
❷ 表達疑問
❸ 表達情緒
❹ 表達否定
❺ 生活用語

★ It's my pleasure...

這是我的榮幸...

用法

完整句型為It's my pleasure to +V(原形動詞).

例句

例 It's my pleasure to meet you.
我很榮幸認識你。

例 It's my pleasure to work with you.
和你一起工作是我的榮幸。

例 It's my pleasure to join your team.
我很榮幸加入你的團隊。

例 It's my pleasure to have dinner with you.
與你共進晚餐是我的榮幸。

★ It's no use+Ving...

...沒有用

用法

完整句型為It's no use + Ving.此句型也等於There is no use+ Ving.或是It's useless + Ving/ to + V (原形動詞).

例句

🔘 It's no use talking with her.
跟她説是沒有用的。

🔘 It's no use explaining the reason to him.
向他解釋理由是沒有用的。

🔘 It's no use telling him the truth.
跟他説實話是沒有用的。

🔘 It's no use crying over spilt milk.
覆水難收。

★ It's rude to...

...是無禮的

完整句型為 It's rude to + V(原形動詞).也可說成
It's impolite to + V(原形動詞).此句中的 rude 是指
"粗魯或莽撞的",而 impolite 則是 "不禮貌
的"。

例 It's rude to cut in line.
插隊是很無禮的。

例 It's rude to yell in public.
在大庭廣眾下大叫是無禮的。

例 It's rude to ask her such a question.
問她這樣的問題是無禮的。

例 It's rude to interrupt when someone is speaking.
在別人講話時插嘴是不禮貌的。

★ It's urgent that...

...是緊急的

用法

完整句型為It's urgent that S+V.或是為It's urgent
to + V(原形動詞).

例句

例 It's urgent that she needs a doctor.
她現在情況危急需要醫生。

例 It's urgent that I must go home now.
情況緊急，我現在必須趕緊回家。

例 It's urgent that we have to do something.
情況緊急，我們必須想辦法解決。

例 It's urgent that you need to send him away.
情況緊急，你現在把他送走。

★ It's wrong to...

是錯的

用法

完整句型為It's wrong to+ V(原形動詞).也可寫成
It's wrong that S+V.

例句

例 It's wrong to do this thing.
這麼做是錯的。

例 It's wrong to tell a lie.
說謊是錯的。

例 It's wrong to tell him the answer.
這樣告訴他答案是錯的。

例 It's wrong to hit people.
打人是錯的。

★ No matter what...

不管怎樣...

用法

> 完整句型為No matter what S+V, S+V.而no matter
> what又可替換成whatever，句型結構也相同。

例句

🅔 No matter what he says, don't trust him.

無論他說什麼，都不要相信他。

🅔 No matter what they do, it's not my business.

無論他們怎麼做，都不關我的事。

🅔 No matter what you say, I won't change my mind.

無論你說什麼，我都不會改變我的心意。

🅔 No matter what my parents say, I still love you.

無論我父母怎麼說，我還是愛你。

① 轉折連結
② 表達疑問
③ 表達情緒
④ 表達否定
⑤ 生活用語

136

★ not to mention...

更別提...

用法

完整句型為 S+V, not to mention+ N. 此句也等於
It's without saying that S+V.

例句

例 I don't like reading, not to mention tests.
我不喜歡讀書，更別說考試了。

例 I'm not willing to do it, not to mention Paul.
我都不願意做這事了，更別說保羅了。

例 He likes sports, not to mention basketball.
他喜歡運動，更別說是籃球了。

例 He doesn't listen to what I say, not to mention you.
他都不聽我說的，更別說你了。

★ take+N+ for granted...

視...為理所當然

❶ 轉折連結
❷ 表達疑問
❸ 表達情緒
❹ 表達否定
❺ 生活用語

用法

完整句型為 S+ take+ N+ for granted that +S+V.
有時候也可只說到 S+ take+ N+ for granted. 視說
話者所要表達之意而定。

例句

例 Don't take it for granted.
別把它視為理所當然。

例 Don't take anything for granted.
別把任何事視為理所當然。

例 Don't take other's help for granted.
別把別人的幫助視為理所當然。

例 Most people take this matter for granted.
大部分的人都視這件事為理所當然。

★ Thank God that...

感謝老天爺...

用法

> 完整句型為Thank God that S+V.此句中的God要
> 大寫，須注意。

例句

例 Thank God that I can go now.
感謝老天爺我現在可以走了。

例 Thank God that it's Friday.
感謝老天爺終於星期五了。

例 Thank God that I made it!
感謝老天爺我成功了！

例 Thank God that I finished the work.
感謝老天爺我完成這工作了。

★ the...S have ever...

...是我有史以來...

用法

完整句型為Someone/Something +be動詞+最高級
形容詞+N+ S+V.這裡的動詞要用現在完成式表
示,因為句中有have ever(表示從以前到現在之
意)。

例句

例 This is the best thing I have ever done.
這是我有史以來做過最棒的事了。

例 This is best food I have ever eaten.
這是我吃過最好吃的食物了。

例 She is the most beautiful girl I have ever
met.
她是我遇過最美的女生了。

例 He is the tallest man I have ever seen.
他是我見過身高最高的人。

❶ 轉折連結

❷ 表達疑問

❸ 表達情緒

❹ 表達否定

❺ 生活用語

★ This is why...

這就是為什麼...

用法

完整句型為 This is why S+V. 此句型原為 This is
the reason why S+V. 因此句中的 the reason 可加可
不加，不會影響其句意。

例句

例 This is why I can't tell you.
這就是為什麼我不能告訴你的原因。

例 This is why I feel disappointed.
這就是為什麼我失望的原因。

例 This is why he is so angry.
這就是為什麼他如此生氣的原因。

例 This is why she can't come today.
這就是為什麼她今天不能來的原因。

★ To my disappointment, ...

讓我失望的是...

用法

> 完整句型為To my disappointment, S+V.這裡的my 也可改為其他所有格，例如：your, his, her, our, their或是人名's—Mark's。

例句

🔲 To my disappointment, he lied to me.
讓我失望的是，他騙了我。

🔲 To my disappointment, she failed the exam.
讓我感到失望的是，她考試沒過。

🔲 To my disappointment, you left without saying goodbye.
讓我失望的是，你不告而別。

🔲 To my disappointment, you gave up halfway.
讓我失望的是，你中途放棄。

❶ 轉折連結
❷ 表達疑問
❸ 表達情緒
❹ 表達否定
❺ 生活用語

★ To my surprise, ...

讓我驚訝的是...

用法

完整句型為To my surprise, S+V.其結構如同前一
組句型，由此可知to+所有格+情緒名詞。

例句

例 To my surprise, he made it.
讓我驚訝的是，他成功了。

例 To my surprise, he knew the answer.
讓我驚訝的是，他居然知道答案。

例 To my surprise, she didn't get angry.
讓我驚訝的是，她竟然沒生氣。

例 To my surprise, they agreed to the plan.
讓我驚訝的是，他們同意了這項計畫。

★ What concerns me is...

我所擔心心/關心的是...

用法

完整句型為What concerns me is +N.或是What I concern is +疑問詞+S+V,其中的疑問詞可為what/when/where/who/how等。

例句

🗨 What concerns me is your safety.
我所擔心的是你的安全。

🗨 What concerns me is my mom's health.
我所擔心的是我媽的健康。

🗨 What concerns me is who did this.
我所關心的是誰做了這件事。

🗨 What concerns me is how you feel about the plan.
我所關心的是你覺得這計畫如何。

★ You are supposed to...

你應該...

完整句型為 You are supposed to +V(原形動詞).這裡的 supposed to 不可分開，須合在一起使用。

例 You are supposed to be here.
你應該在這裡的。

例 You are supposed to say sorry to her.
你應該剛她道歉的。

例 You are supposed to call me.
你應該打電話給我。

例 You are supposed to stay at home.
你應該待在家裡。

★ You drive me...

你讓我...

完整句型為 You drive me +Adj.常用形容詞有 crazy, mad 等。

例 You drive me crazy.
你讓我為之瘋狂。

例 You drive me mad.
你讓我太生氣了。

例 You drive me nuts.
你讓我快發瘋了。

例 You drive me bananas.
你讓我發瘋了。

❶ 轉折連結
❷ 表達疑問
❸ 表達情緒
❹ 表達否定
❺ 生活用語

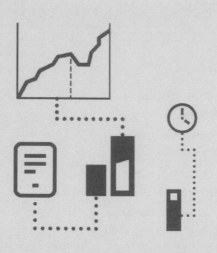

Chapter 4

表達否定

★ S could no longer+V...

　再也不能...

完整句型為S could no longer +V(原形動詞).此句
等於S couldn't +V (原形動詞)+any longer.

例 I could no longer come here.
　我再也不能來這裡了。

例 I could no longer see you.
　我再也不能見到你了。

例 He could no longer work in the company.
　他再也不能在公司工作了。

例 They could no longer hurt you.
　他們再也不能傷害你了。

★ S hardly+V...

幾乎不...

用法

完整句型為S+ hardly +V(原形動詞).這裡的hardly 已經有否定的意思，所以不要再加no或not等否 定的字詞。

例句

例 I could hardly stand upright.
我幾乎無法站直。

例 I could hardly believe it.
我簡直不敢相信這事。

例 I could hardly breathe.
我幾乎無法呼吸。

例 He could hardly win the game.
他幾乎要輸掉這場比賽。

★ S will never+V...

絕不...

完整句型為S+ will never +V(原形動詞)，表示
"絕不" 之意。

例 I will never see him again.
我絕不會再見他一面。

例 I will never do it.
我絕不會做這件事。

例 I will never go there.
我絕不會去那裡。

例 I will never eat this kind of food.
我絕不會吃這種食物。

★ Don't be+Adj....

不要...

用法

完整句型為 Don't be +Adj.(形容詞).若要加強語
氣,可加上 so 或 too,即為 Don't be+ so/too +
Adj.。

例句

例 Don't be mad.
不要生氣。

例 Don't be so childish.
不要這麼幼稚了。

例 Don't be too tired.
別太累。

例 Don't be harsh on him.
別對他太嚴苛。

① 轉折連結
② 表達疑問
③ 表達情緒
④ 表達否定
⑤ 生活用語

★ Don't let S+V...

別讓...

完整句型為Don't let S+V(原形動詞)。由於let是使役動詞，所以let後面的動詞須為原形動詞。

例 Don't let him go away.
別讓他逃走。

例 Don't let him see me.
別讓他看到我。

例 Don't let her eat too much.
別讓她吃太多。

例 Don't let Adam come here.
別讓亞當來這裡。

★I can't accept+N...

我不能接受...

用法

完整句型為 I can't accept +N.或為 I can't accept that+S+V.抑或 I can't accept what S+V.

例句

例 I can't accept the truth.

我不能接受這事實。

例 I can't accept your present.

我不能接受你的禮物。

例 I can't accept what she said.

我不能接受她所說的。

例 I can't accept that he lost the game.

我不能接受他輸了這場比賽。

❶轉折連結

❷表達疑問

❸表達情緒

❹表達否定

❺生活用語

★ I can't believe...

我無法相信...

完整句型為 I can't believe + N.或是 I can't believe that S+V.抑或 I can't believe what S+V.

例 I can't believe it.
　　我無法相信這事。

例 I can't believe the news.
　　我無法相信這消息。

例 I can't believe what they said.
　　我無法相信他們所說的。

例 I can't believe that he did this to you.
　　我無法相信他對你這麼做。

★ I can't do...

我不能做...

 用法

完整句型為I can't do + V(原形動詞).其後可加一
些片語或副詞來修飾句子。

 例句

📢 I can't do that.
　我不能那麼做。

📢 I can't do it alone.
　我無法單獨做這事。

📢 I can't do it without your support.
　沒有你的支持,我無法做這件事。

📢 I can't do it without my mom's permission.
　未經我媽的允許,我不能做這事。

① 轉折連結　② 表達疑問　③ 表達情緒　④ 表達否定　⑤ 生活用語

★ I can't help...

我不得不...

完整句型為I can't help +Ving.此句型等於I can't help but +V(原形動詞)./I can't but + V(原形動詞)./I have no choice but to + V(原形動詞).

例 I can't help seeing the movie.
我不得不去看那場電影。

例 I can't help staring at the girl.
我無法停止不盯著那女生看。

例 I can't help finishing the work.
我不得不完成這工作。

例 I can't help telling the lie to her.
我不得不對她說謊。

★ I can't imagine...

我無法想像...

用法

完整句型為I can't imagine +N.也可寫成I can't
imagine +疑問詞(5W1H)+S+V.或是I can't imagine
that S+V.

例句

例 I can't imagine that picture.
我無法想像那畫面。

例 I can't imagine her pain.
我無法想像她的痛苦。

例 I can't imagine what has happened.
我無法想像發生了什麼事。

例 I can't imagine what they did to him.
我無法想像他們對他所做的。

① 轉折連結
② 表達疑問
③ 表達情緒
④ 表達否定
⑤ 生活用語

★ I can't stop...

我不能停止...

完整句型為I can't stop + Ving/N.這裡的動詞須加上ing，表示停止之意。若寫成stop to +V(原形動詞)，則表示"停下來，而去做某事"之意，所以兩者句意不同。

例 I can't stop him.
　　我無法制止他。

例 I can't stop the machine.
　　我無法使這機器停下來。

例 I can't stop loving you.
　　我無法不愛你。

例 I can't stop doing it.
　　我無法停止做這件事。

★I couldn't let you...

我不能讓你...

用法

完整句型為I couldn't let you +V(原形動詞).這裡的let是使役動詞，所以其後的動詞須為原形動詞的形式。

例句

例 I couldn't let you go.
我不能讓你走。

例 I couldn't let you stay here alone.
我不能讓你獨自待在這裡。

例 I couldn't let you feel disappointed.
我不能讓你感到失望。

例 I couldn't let you do this thing.
我不能讓你做這件事。

❶ 轉折連結

❷ 表達疑問

❸ 表達情緒

❹ 表達否定

❺ 生活用語

★ I didn't...

我沒有...

用法

完整句型為I didn't + V (原形動詞).此句用在當
別人對你所說或所做之事,有誤解時,因為是當
時別人認為你所做的,但你為了要解釋當時的情
況,動詞就要用過去式。

例句

例 I didn't do it.
我沒有做這事。

例 I didn't go home yesterday.
我昨天沒回家。

例 I didn't lie.
我沒有說謊。

例 I didn't go to school this morning.
我今天早上沒去上學。

★ I don't care...

我不在乎...

用法

完整句型為I don't care about +N/Ving.或為I don't care +疑問詞(5W1H)+S+V.

例句

例 I don't care about him.
我才不在乎他。

例 I don't care about the matter.
我不在乎這件事。

例 I don't care what they say.
我不在乎他們所說的。

例 I don't care what you do.
我不在乎你所做的。

★I don't know how to...

> 我不知該如何...

完整句型為I don't know how to +V (原形動詞).

例 I don't know how to do it.

我不知道該如何做這事。

例 I don't know how to solve the problem.

我不知道該如何解決這問題。

例 I don't know how to talk with her.

我不知道該如何跟她說。

例 I don't know how to face him.

我不知道該如何面對他。

★ I didn't know...

我不知道...

用法

完整句型為I didn't know that S+V.也可寫成I didn't know +N.或是I didn't know+疑問詞+S+V.

例句

⑩ I didn't know that he is your dad.
我不知道他是你爸爸。

⑩ I didn't know that you like her.
我不知道你喜歡她。

⑩ I didn't know that you moved here.
我不知道你搬來這裡。

⑩ I didn't know that she went home.
我不知道她回家了。

★ I don't like...

我不喜歡...

用法

> 完整句型為 I don't like + N/ to+V.或為 I don't like+ what/how +S+V.

例句

例 I don't like your haircut.
我不喜歡你的髮型。

例 I don't like his friends.
我不喜歡他的朋友。

例 I don't like to go out.
我不喜歡出門。

例 I don't like to do homework.
我不喜歡做功課。

★ I don't mind...

我不介意...

用法

完整句型為I don't mind that S+V./I don't mind + Ving/N.

例句

例 I don't mind your background.
我不介意你的背景。

例 I don't mind standing here.
我不介意站在這裡。

例 I don't mind that you open the window.
我不介意你打開窗戶。

例 I don't mind that you borrow my notes.
我不介意你跟我借筆記。

★ I don't think...

我不認為...

完整句型為 I don't think that S+V. 這裡要注意的是，不可以把 not 放在 that 子句裡，例如：I think she is not the thief.(×)。

而應改成 I don't think she is the thief.(我不認為她是小偷。)

例 I don't think he is right.
　我不認為他是對的。

例 I don't think she can do the work.
　我不認為她可以做這工作。

例 I don't think we should leave here.
　我不認為我們該離開這裡。

例 I don't think you should follow the rule.
　我不認為你該照著這規則。

★ I don't understand...

我不懂...

用法

完整句型為 I don't understand +N. 或是 I don't understand why S+V.

例句

 I don't understand the question.
我不懂這問題。

 I don't understand your point.
我不懂你的重點。

例 I don't understand why he gave up.
我不懂為何他放棄。

例 I don't understand why she left.
我不懂為何她要離開。

★ I failed to...

我無法...

完整句型為 I failed to +V(原形動詞).雖然fail有
失敗之意但在這裡是當作 "無法或沒有" 之意
解。

例

例 I failed to pass the test.

我沒有通過測驗。

例 I failed to finish the work.

我沒有完成這工作。

例 I failed to hand in my homework before
Friday.

我沒有在星期五前繳交功課。

例 I failed to break the record.

我沒有破紀錄。

★I have no idea about...

我不知道...

 用法

完整句型為I have no idea about +N/Ving.或為 I have no idea about+ what to+ V(原形動詞)/how to + V(原形動詞).

 例句

例 I have no idea about this matter.
我不知道這件事情。

例 I have no idea about solving the problem.
我不知道該怎麼解決這問題。

例 I have no idea what to do.
我不知道該怎麼做。

例 I have no idea about how to answer his question.
我不知道該怎麼回答他的問題。

★ I haven't...

我還沒...

完整句型為 I haven't+Vpp(完成式).後面可以再加 yet(用在完成式裡的否定句)，不加也可。

例 I haven't had dinner.
我還沒吃晚餐。

例 I haven't finished my homework.
我還沒寫完作業。

例 I haven't been there yet.
我還沒去過那裡。

例 I haven't told her the news.
我還沒告訴她消息。

★ I shouldn't...
我不該...

完整句型為 I shouldn't +V(原形動詞).此句也可寫成 I'm not supposed to+V(原形動詞).

例句

例 I shouldn't trust him.
我不該相信他的。

例 I shouldn't let her go.
我不該讓她走的。

例 I shouldn't give up.
我不該放棄的。

例 I shouldn't go out with my brother.
我不該跟我哥出去的。

❶ 轉折連結
❷ 表達疑問
❸ 表達情緒
❹ 表達否定
❺ 生活用語

★ I try not to...

我試著不去...

用法

完整句型為I try not to+V(原形動詞).這裡要注意
的是，大多數人會忽略to(因為try是動詞，其後
若要再接動詞，要將to置於兩動詞之間)。

例句

例 I try not to cry.
我試著不哭。

例 I try not to let her go.
我試著不讓她離開。

例 I try not to think about him.
我試著不去想他。

例 I try not to give up.
我試著不要放棄。

★ I won't...

我不會...

用法

完整句型為 I won't+V (原形動詞).這裡的 won't 有
向對方保證的意思，表示承諾對方不會做某事。

例句

例 I won't cry.
我不會哭的。

例 I won't hurt you.
我不會傷害你的。

例 I won't give up.
我不會放棄的。

例 I won't let you down.
我不會讓你失望的。

★ I'm not sure that...

我不確定...

完整句型為I'm not sure if S+V.句中的sure也可用certain(確定的)替換，意思皆同。

例 I'm not sure that I can do it.
我不確定我可以做這事。

例 I'm not sure that he is sick.
我不確定他是否生病。

例 I'm not sure that he will come.
我不確定他會不會來。

例 I'm not sure that she will accept me.
我不確定她是否會接受我。

★ It's not necessary...

沒有必要...

完整句型為It's not necessary to+ V(原形動詞).此
句也可寫成It's unnecessary to+ V(原形動詞).

例 It's not necessary to help him.
沒有必要幫他。

例 It's not necessary to tell her the truth.
沒有必要告訴她事實。

例 It's not necessary to give him money.
沒有必要給他錢。

例 It's not necessary to send her a gift.
沒有必要送她禮物。

★ I've never...

我從來沒...

完整句型為I've never +V(完成式).因為句中有have (在此為助動詞)，所以動詞要用完成式。

例 I've never been there.
我從未去過那裡。

例 I've never seen the boy.
我從未看過那男孩。

例 I've never seen that movie.
我從未看過那部電影。

例 I've never heard the news.
我從未聽過這消息。

★ Neither...nor...

既不是...也不是...

完整句型為Neither A nor B+V.這裡的動詞型態
要以最靠近的主詞為主,來做變化,例如:Nei-
ther he nor she wants this gift.(他和她都不想要
這禮物)。

例 Neither she nor I knew the news.
　　我和她都不知道這消息。

例 Neithr Sally nor Sarah did it.
　　這件事不是莎莉也不是莎拉做的。

例 Neither Simon nor Sherry can swim.
　　賽蒙和雪莉都不會游泳。

例 Neither he nor she likes work.
　　他和她都不喜歡工作。

★ No one knows...

沒人知道...

用法

完整句型為No one knows＋N.或是No one knows that S＋V.抑或No one knows＋疑問詞＋to ＋V(原形動詞)。這裡的know於現在式中要加上s，因為no one是當作第三人稱單數。

例句

例 No one knows him.
沒人認識他。

例 No one knows the secret.
沒人知道這秘密。

例 No one knows his real name.
沒人知道他真正的姓名。

例 No one knows how to do it.
沒人知道該怎麼處理這件事。

★ No one+V...

沒有人...

用法

完整句型為No one +Vs/Ves/Vpt+N.句中的動詞可使用現在式或過去式，若為現在式，其動詞要加上s或es。

例句

例 No one likes the smell.
沒人喜歡那味道。

例 No one passed the exam.
沒人通過考試。

例 No one answered the phone.
沒人接電話。

例 No one came here yesterday.
昨天沒有人來這裡。

★ No+Ving...

不可以；禁止...

用法

完整句型為No+Ving.原本句型為 There is no + Ving.通常這樣的句子會用在警告性的標語上，例如，禁止奔跑、禁止抽菸等。

例句

例 No running.
禁止奔跑。

例 No smoking.
禁止抽菸。

例 No entering.
禁止進入。

例 No littering.
勿亂丟垃圾。

★ None of+N...

沒有一個...

用法

完整句型為None of +N+V.句中的主詞就是none，為代名詞，視為第三人稱單數名詞。句中的N為複數名詞，但動詞卻為單數形，要加上s或es，須特別注意。

例句

例 None of them speaks English.
他們都不會講英語。

例 None of my friends smokes.
我的朋友們都不抽菸。

例 None of us knows the answer.
我們都不知道答案。

例 None of the computers is working.
沒有一台電腦可以用。

★ not...anymore/ longer...

再也不...

用法

> 完整句型為 S +not +V+ anymore/longer. 句中的動
> 詞可為現在式或過去式，視說話者所表達之意而
> 定。

例句

例 I don't love him anymore.

我再也不愛他了。

例 I can't stand her anymore.

我再也受不了她了。

例 I can't do it any longer.

我再也不能這麼做了。

例 She doesn't work here any longer.

她不再在這裡工作了。

★ Please don't...

請不要...

用法

完整句型為Please don't+ V(原形動詞).加上please
較有禮貌,若不加please,則屬於命令式的語氣,
語意就明顯不同。而主詞部分其實是"You"的
省略,因為通常這樣的句型就是在跟對方講話,
所以沒有必要再加上"You"。

例句

例 Please don't go.
請不要走。

例 Please don't cry.
請不要哭。

例 Please don't do it.
請不要這樣做。

例 Please don't touch my book.
請不要碰我的書。

轉折連結 ❶ 表達疑問 ❷ 表達情緒 ❸ 表達否定 ❹ 生活用語 ❺

★ That can't be…

那不可能…

完整句型為 That can't be+ Adj.(形容詞)/N(名詞).
當對方告訴你某事情或消息時，而你覺得不可能
會是那樣子，或是你不相信的時候，就可用此句
表達。

例 That can't be right.

　那不可能是正確的。

例 That can't be true.

　那不可能是真的。

例 That can't be so easy.

　那不會那麼簡單的。

例 That can't be mine.

　那不會是我的。

★ That is not...

那不是...

用法

完整句型為That is not+ N(單數名詞)+(to +V).此句常用在對方問你此物是不是你的，或者某事是不是你負責的時候，就可以用此句型回答。

例句

例 That is not my business.
那不關我的事。

例 That is not my book.
那不是我的書。

例 That is not my first time to do it.
我不是第一次這麼做了。

例 That is not my duty to clean the room.
打掃這間房間不是我的責任。

★ That makes no difference...

...沒有差別

用法

完整句型為That makes no difference to+人(受詞)+(whether S+V or not).若說話者想表達更仔細的語意，就可用上句中括號的部分。whether為"是否"之意。

例句

例 That makes no difference to me.

那對我而言沒有差別。

例 That makes no difference to those rich men.

那對有錢人而言沒有差別。

例 That makes no difference to her whether Tom comes or not.

湯姆是否有來，對她而言沒有差別。

例 That makes no difference to me whether he finds a job or not.

他是否找到工作，對我而言沒有差別。

Chapter 5

生活用語

★ ...as well

也...

用法

完整句型為S+V and S+V as well.此處的as well 等於too(也)，皆用於肯定句和疑問句，且置於句尾，不同處在於too前面會加逗點。例如：Sandy likes ice cream and I like it as well. = Sandy likes ice cream and I like it, too. (珊迪喜歡冰淇淋，我也喜歡。)

例句

例 He is leaving and I am leaving as well.
他要離開，我也要離開。

例 David is hungry and Kevin is hungry as well.
大衛餓了，凱文也餓了。

例 Do you want to join us as well?
你也想加入我們嗎？

例 Do you want to play basketball as well?
你也想打籃球嗎？

★ ...by chance

偶然、意外...

完整句型為S+V by chance.這裡的by chance等於
accidentally(意外地)。通常用於所發生過的事，因
此動詞用過去式表示。

I met Bruce by chance last night.
我昨晚巧遇布魯斯。

His success was not by chance.
他的成功不是偶然的。

The car accident happened by chance.
這場車禍是意外所致。

I found the diary by chance.
我意外發現這本日記。

★ ...do harm to+N

...對...有害

用法

完整句型為S+ do harm to +N.這裡的do可以視
主詞的情況(單數或複數)，改成does或是do。此
句也等於A+ be動詞+harmful to+ B。例如：
Smoking does harm to our health. = Smoking is
harmful to our health.(抽菸有害健康。)

例
句

例 Drinking too much does harm to you.
　 飲酒過多會對你有害。

例 Does the medicine do harm to us?
　 這藥對我們有害嗎？

例 The news will do harm to our company.
　 這消息會對我們公司不利。

例 It won't do harm to you.
　 它不會對你有害。

★ ...er than...

比...

用法

完整句型為 A is/are+比較級形容詞+than +B.例如：He is taller than I. (他比我高。)或是 A+V+比較級形容詞+than +B。例如：He runs faster than I.(他跑得比我快。)

例句

例 Helen is cuter than my sister.
海倫比我妹還可愛。

例 Frank is fatter than George.
法蘭克比喬治還胖。

例 Sam walks slower than Leo.
山姆走得比李歐還慢。

例 My mom cooks better than my dad.
我媽煮得比我爸還好。

❷
❷
❶
❶ 轉折連結
❷ 表達疑問
❸ 表達情緒
❹ 表達否定
❺ 生活用語

★ ...for a long time

...很久...

完整句型為S+V for a long time.因為for a long
time表示一段長時間,所以此句型通常用於現在
完成式,例如:I have studied English for a long
time. (我讀英文很久了。)

⑩ I have known him for a long time.
   我已經認識他很久了。

⑩ I have lived here for a long time.
   我已經住在這裡很久了。

⑩ She has learned music for a long time.
   她學音樂學很久了。

⑩ I haven't seen him for a long time.
   我很久沒看見他了。

★ A and B both...

A 和 B 兩個都...

完整句型為 A and B both+複數動詞.也可等於 Both A and B+複數動詞。由於句中有 both 這個字，所以只能用於兩者身上，例如：Walter and Ruby both are my friends.(瓦特和盧比都是我的朋友。)或是 Both Bill and Ted did well. (比爾和泰德都做得很好。)三者以上則用 all。

例 Gary and Steven both are my best friends.
蓋瑞和史蒂芬都是我最好的朋友。

例 Music and movies both are my hobbies.
音樂和電影都是我的嗜好。

例 Both Jack and Jason are my brothers.
傑克和傑生都是我的兄弟。

例 Both you and she performed well.
你和她都表現得很好。

❶ 轉折連結
❷ 表達疑問
❸ 表達情緒
❹ 表達否定
❺ 生活用語

★ a bit+Adj....

有一點...

完整句型為S+ be動詞/V + a bit Adj.(形容詞).而
a bit= a little，後面都加形容詞。

例 I feel a bit dizzy.

我頭有點暈。

例 The room is a bit small.

這間房間有點小。

例 This question is a bit difficult.

這個問題有點難。

例 Your clothes are a bit dirty.

你的衣服有點髒。

★ A convince B of+N/ that...

A 説服 B...

用法

> 完整句型為A convince B of +N.或是A convince B that S+V.

例句

例 He convinced me of his correct decision.
他讓我相信他的決定是正確的。

例 She convinced me of her innocence.
她讓我相信她是無辜的。

例 He convinced me that he made a right decision.
他讓我相信他所做的決定是正確的。

例 She convinced me that she was innocent.
她讓我相信她是無辜的。

❶ 轉折連結

❷ 表達疑問

❸ 表達情緒

❹ 表達否定

❺ 生活用語

★ A have B...

A 叫 B...

用法

完整句型為 A have/has/had B+V(原形動詞)。由於這裡的 have 為使役動詞，所以其後的動詞要用原形動詞，表示主動；若為 Vpp(過去分詞)，則表示被動。

例句

例 My mom has me do the dishes every day.
　我媽每天都叫我洗碗。

例 He has me do exercise every day.
　他勸我每天要運動。

例 I had my computer repaired.
　我把我的電腦送修。

例 I had Tom repair my computer.
　我叫湯姆幫我修電腦。

★ S is busy+Ving...

...忙著...

用法

完整句型為S+be動詞+busy+ Ving.此句中的busy
後面一定要加進行式(Vng)的動詞。另外，busy後
面若要接名詞，介系詞須用 with，即 beV+busy
with+N.

例句

例 I am busy doing my homework.
我正忙著寫工作。

例 I am busy working now.
我正忙著工作。

例 She is busy cooking.
她正忙著煮飯。

例 He is busy preparing his report.
他正忙著準備他的報告。

★ S is going to+V...

...就要...

用法

完整句型為S+ beV+ going to +V(原形動詞).此句型是用於已經事先計劃好並決定按計畫實行的情況，且通常有確切時間。

例
句

例 I am going to leave tomorrow.
我明天就要離開了。

例 I am going to see the movie later.
我待會就要去看電影了。

例 My train is going to leave in ten minutes.
我的火車十分鐘內就要駛離了。

例 She is going to visit Frank this weekend.
她這個周末就會去拜訪法蘭克。

★ S is good at+N...

...擅長...

完整句型為 S+ be動詞+good at +N/Ving. 此句中的 at 為介系詞，所以動詞要加 ing.

例 I am good at English.
我擅長英文。

例 I am good at cooking.
我擅長烹飪。

例 She is good at computers.
她擅長電腦。

例 He is good at basketball.
他擅長打籃球。

★ A is good for B...

A 對 B 有益處...

用法

完整句型為A+ is/are good for+ B. 句中的A和B
須為名詞形態(包含動名詞)。A若為複數形,動
詞用are;但若A為單數名詞或是動名詞,後面的
動詞就要用單數形。

例句

例 Exercise is good for our health.
運動對我們的健康有益。

例 Vegetables and fruits are good for us.
蔬果對我們有益。

例 Reading is good for you.
閱讀對你有益。

例 Drinking milk is good for your health.
喝牛奶有益你的健康。

★ A is related to B...

A 和 B 有關...

用法

完整句型為A+ is/are related to+ B.句中的A和B
皆為名詞。

例句

🔹 This matter is related to Peter.
這件事和彼得有關。

🔹 That man is related to the car accident.
那個男人跟這場車禍有關。

🔹 Those files are related to the case.
那些檔案和這個案件有關。

🔹 These people are related to the group.
這些人和那個團體有關。

★ S is responsible for...

對...負責

用法

完整句型為S + is/are responsible for + N.此句的
be動詞(is 或是 are)，須視主詞而定。

例句

📙 I am responsible for my mistakes.
我會對我犯的錯負責。

📙 He is responsible for the case.
他會對這個案件負責。

📙 We are responsible for the result.
我們都要對這個結果負責。

📙 They are responsible for the plan.
他們要對這項計畫負責。

★ S is situated in...

...位於...

完整句型為 S is/are situated in+N. 句中的 N 為一地點。另外，beV situated in=beV located in=lie in。

例 Taipei 101 is situated in Taiwan.
　 台北101位於台灣。

例 New York is situated in America.
　 紐約位於美國。

例 Her house is situated in the downtown area.
　 她家位在市中心。

例 That shopping mall is situated in the suburbs.
　 那家購物中心位於郊區。

① 轉折連結　② 表達疑問　③ 表達情緒　④ 表達否定　⑤ 生活用語

201

track 5-9

★ A is the same as B...

A 和 B 一樣...

用法

完整句型為 A+ beV the same as+ B.句中的 the same as 通常都合在一起使用，須注意。而 A 和 B 須為相同性質的東西才能比較。另外，same 是完全一樣，而 similar 則是類似、相像而已。

例句

例 My book is the same as yours.
我的書和你的一樣。

例 Your cell phone is the same as mine.
你的手機和我的一樣。

例 His birthday is the same as hers.
他的生日和她同一天。

例 My score is the same as yours.
我和你同分。

★ S is what we call...

...就是我們所謂的...

用法

完整句型為S is what we call +N.通常這種句型
會用現在式，表示已成為常態的說法。

例句

⑩ That is what we call "art".

那就是我們所說的 "藝術"。

⑩ This is what we call "the power of love".

這就是我們所說的 "愛的力量"。

⑩ That kind of man is what we call
"genius".

那種人就是我們所謂的 "天才"。

⑩ He is what we call "a walking dictionary".

他就是我們所說的 "活字典"。

203

★ S keep...

...持續...

用法

完整句型為S+ keep+(B)+ Ving/Adj.句中的B即為
受詞，可加可不加，視說話者所欲表達之意而
定。

例句

例 He kept asking me questions.
他一直問我問題。

例 He kept walking forward.
他一直向前走。

例 He kept the students quiet.
他讓學生保持安靜。

例 That joke kept me laughing.
那個笑話一直讓我發笑。

★ A make B...

A 讓 B...

完整句型為 A make B +Adj./V(原形動詞).句中的 make為使役動詞,所以動詞是原形動詞。

例 He always makes me angry.
他總是讓我生氣。

例 Eating makes me happy.
吃會讓我感到快樂。

例 The story makes me feel sad.
這個故事讓我感到悲傷。

例 My mom makes me do homework every day.
我媽每天叫我要寫功課。

① 轉折連結 ② 表達疑問 ③ 表達情緒 ④ 表達否定 ⑤ 生活用語

★ S need to+V/N...

...需要...

完整句型為S need to +V(原形動詞).或是S need +N.

例 I need money.
我需要錢。

例 I need a job.
我需要一份工作。

例 I need to go now.
我現在就得走了。

例 I need to make a call.
我需要打通電話。

★ a number of+N...

許多...

完整句型為S+V+ a number of +N(複數名詞).或為 A number of+ N(複數名詞)+V(複數形).從句型可知,a number of可放句中或句首,而所接的名詞須為複數名詞,動詞也是複數形(a number of 放句首時)。

> 例 Larry has a number of books.
> 賴瑞有許多本書。

> 例 Mr. Lai has a number of houses.
> 賴先生有許多棟房子。

> 例 A number of people believe the news.
> 許多人相信這消息。

> 例 A number of students don't like tests.
> 許多學生都不喜歡考試。

英語句型 這樣學 才會快

207 　　　　　　　🎧 track 5-12

★ A remind B of...

A 提醒 B...

用法

> 完整句型為 A remind B of+ N/ to+V(原形動詞).
> 或是 A remind B that S+V.

例句

例 The story reminds me of my family.
那個故事讓我想起我的家人。

例 The picture reminds me of my childhood.
這張照片讓我想起我的童年。

例 My mom always reminds me to study hard.
我媽總是提醒我要用功讀書。

例 Our boss often reminds us to work hard.
我們老闆常常提醒我們要努力工作。

★ S sit/stand/lie...

...坐/站/躺著...

用法

完整句型為 S sit/stand/lie+ Ving.這裡的動詞要加上 ing，屬於特定用法，須特別注意。

例句

例 She lies watching TV.
她躺著看電視。

例 She stands reading a book.
她站著看書。

例 You should sit having a meal.
你應該坐著用餐。

例 He often stands eating breakfast.
他常站著吃早餐。

★ S tend to...

...傾向於...

完整句型為 S tend to+N/V(原形動詞).句中的 to 也
可用 towards。另外，tend to=have a tendency to=
have an inclination to.

例 I tend to your plan.
　我傾向用你的計畫。

例 He tends to that group.
　他傾向那一組。

例 He tends to become fat.
　他有發福的傾向。

例 She tends to get angry.
　她好像要生氣的感覺。

★ adapt oneself to...

適應...

用法

完整句型為S+adapt oneself to+ Ving/N.這裡的to 為介系詞，所以動詞要加ing，也視為特定用法。

例句

例 I adapt myself to the new teacher.
我讓自己去適應那位新老師。

例 I adapt myself to forgetting him.
我調整自己來忘記他。

例 She adapted herself to the hot weather.
她讓自己去適應這炎熱的天氣。

例 He tried to adapt himself to the company.
他試著讓自己適應那間公司。

① 轉折連結　② 表達疑問　③ 表達情緒　④ 表達否定　⑤ 生活用語

★ After+N/Ving,...

在...之後

用法

完整句型為After+ N/Ving, S+V.此句的句型原為
After S+V,S+V.在主詞相同情況下,為了避免主詞
的重複,所以把前者的主詞刪去,動詞則改為
Ving,就會變成After +Ving, S+V的形態。

例句

🈁 After graduation, he went abroad.
畢業之後,他就出國去了。

🈁 After a rest, she became better.
休息過後,她有比較好了。

🈁 After taking a bath, he went to bed.
洗完澡後,他就去睡覺了。

🈁 After hearing the news, she cried.
聽到消息後,她哭了。

★ All I have to do is...

我能做的就是...

完整句型為All I have to do is+V(原形動詞).原句型為All I have to do is to+V.但常會省略to,此為習慣用法,所以須特別注意。

例 All I have to do is wait.
我能做的就是等待。

例 All I have to do is study.
我能做的就是讀書。

例 All I have to do is learn.
我能做的就是學習。

例 All I have to do is work hard.
我能做的就是努力工作。

★ As a/an A,...

身為... , A...

完整句型為 As a/an A, S+V. 此句的 A 為一種身分
的名稱,例如:職業或角色。

📙 As a student, you should study hard.

作為學生,你應該努力讀書。

📙 As a teacher, you should be more patient.

作為老師,你更應該有耐心。

📙 As an employee, you should do your best.

作為一個員工,你應該盡力而為。

📙 As a boss, he should set an example.

作為老闆,他應該以身作則。

★ as possible as S can...

盡...所能地...

用法

完整句型為S+V+ as possible as S can.此句型中，主詞S為同一人。

例句

例 I would finish the work as possible as I can.

我會盡我所能地完成這項工作。

例 I would study hard as possible as I can.

我會盡我所能地努力讀書。

例 He would make money as possible as he can.

他會盡他所能地來賺錢。

例 He would help her as possible as he can.

他會盡他所能地來幫她。

❶ 轉折連結

❷ 表達疑問

❸ 表達情緒

❹ 表達否定

❺ 生活用語

★ as...as...

像...一樣...

用法

完整句型為 A+V+ as Adj.(形容詞)/Adv.(副詞) as+
B.句中的動詞若屬於be動詞或是連綴動詞(如：
feel, sound, smell, look, taste)，就用as Adj.as；
若為一般動詞(如：run, jump, do……等)，就用as
Adv. As。

例句

This house is as tall as that tree.
這棟房子和那棵樹一樣高。

He looks as old as my brother.
他看起來和我哥哥一樣大。

He runs as fast as a horse.
他跑得像馬一樣快。

She cooks as well as my mom.
她煮得跟我一樣好。

★ be able to...

能夠...

用法

完整句型為S+ be able to+V(原形動詞).be able to 就等於can，有"可以、能夠"之意。

例句

例 I am able to speak English.
我會說英文。

例 I am able to swim now.
我現在會游泳了。

例 I am able to finish the work on my own.
我能獨自完成這項工作。

例 Am I able to leave?
我可以走了嗎？

★ be addicted to...

沉溺於...

完整句型為 S+ be addicted to+Ving/N. 句中的 to 為介系詞，所以動詞要加 ing，此為特定用法，要特別注意。

例 He is addicted to drinking.
他對酒精上癮。

例 He is addicted to gambling.
他沉溺於賭博之中。

例 She is addicted to TV.
她對電視入了迷。

例 She is addicted to online games.
她沉溺於線上遊戲中。

★ Be careful not...

小心不要...

完整句型為 Be careful not to +V(原形動詞).此種
句型為祈使句,因為對話的對象就是對方,所以
就不再加主詞You。句中的to常被忽略,須注意。

例 Be careful not to fall ill.
   小心不要生病。

例 Be careful not to drive too fast.
   小心不要開太快。

例 Be careful not to talk aloud.
   注意,說話不要太大聲。

例 Be careful not to overeat.
   注意,不要吃過飽。

❶ 轉折連結　❷ 表達疑問　❸ 表達情緒　❹ 表達否定　❺ 生活用語

219

🎧 track 5-18

★ be dressed in...

穿著...

完整句型為S+ be dressed in+衣物/顏色.也等於
S+ wear +衣物.

例 She is dressed in white.
她穿了白色的衣服。

例 She is dressed in a yellow skirt.
她穿了一件黃色裙子。

例 I am dressed in a blue T-shirt.
我穿了一件藍色的T恤。

例 He is dressed in a black jacket.
他穿了一件黑色夾克。

★ be free from...

免於/遠離...

用法

完整句型為 S+ be free from+ N.

例句

 I want to be free from pressure.
我想遠離壓力。

 He tried to be free from the fight.
他試著遠離這場爭鬥。

例 No one can be free from death.
沒有人可以免於死亡。

例 The house is free from the noisy cities.
這間房子遠離塵囂。

❶ 轉折連結
❷ 表達疑問
❸ 表達情緒
❹ 表達否定
❺ 生活用語

★ be getting...

變得...

用法

完整句型為S+ be getting +Adj.(形容詞).這裡的 getting也可以用becoming替代,只是get比較常用。

例句

例 I am getting hungry.
我開始餓了。

例 She is getting fat.
她變胖了。

例 My dad is getting old.
我爸漸漸老了。

例 He is getting smarter.
他變得比較聰明了。

★ be looking for...

尋找...

用法

完整句型為S+ be looking for+N.句中的 look for+
N=search for+N=seek+N.

例句

例 She is looking for her child.

她正在尋找她的小孩。

例 She is looking for more information.

她正在找更多的資訊。

例 I am looking for my cell phone.

我正在找我的手機。

例 My mom is looking for her glasses.

我媽正在找她的眼鏡。

❶ 轉折連結

❷ 表達疑問

❸ 表達情緒

❹ 表達否定

❺ 生活用語

★ be used to...

習慣...

完整句型為S+ be used to +Ving/N.這裡的to為介系詞，所以動詞要加ing，為特定用法。

例 I am used to getting up early.
我習慣早起。

例 I am used to walking to school.
我習慣走路上學。

例 I am used to the life in a city.
我習慣都市的生活。

例 I am used to the weather here.
我習慣這裡的天氣。

★ Compared with ...

> 和...相比...

完整句型為Compared with+N, S+V.

例 Compared with white, I like black more.
和白色相比,我比較喜歡黑色。

例 Compared with noodles, I prefer rice.
和麵相比,我比較偏好米食。

例 Compared with Wells, Kenny is smarter.
和威爾斯相比,肯尼比較聰明。

例 Compared with this one, that one is better.
和這個相比,那一個比較好。

❶轉折連結 ❷表達疑問 ❸表達情緒 ❹表達否定 ❺生活用語

★ devoted to...

專心於...

用法

完整句型為S+ beV + devoted to+ Ving/N.此句也
等於S+ devote oneself to+ Ving/N.

例句

例 She is devoted to her family.

她投入在她的家庭上。

例 He is devoted to study.

他專心於研究上。

例 He is devoted to finishing the work.

他專心完成那項工作。

例 My brother is devoted to preparing his report.

我哥哥專心準備他的報告。

★ do nothing but...

僅...

完整句型為S+ do/did nothing but+V(原形動詞).
這裡的動詞要用原形動詞,不加to,要特別注意。

例 I did nothing but watch TV all day.
我一整天無所事事,只有看電視。

例 He did nothing but study.
他什麼都沒做,只有讀書。

例 She did nothing but wait for his call.
她什麼都沒做,只乾等著他的電話。

例 They did nothing but stand there.
他們什麼都沒做,只是站在那裡。

★ either...or...

不是...就是...

用法

完整句型為 S+V+ either A or B.或是 Either A or B+V.句中的 A 和 B 的形態須為平行結構，如：名詞對名詞，形容詞對形容詞。而此句所欲表達之意為"只能二選一"或是"其中之一"的意思。

例句

例 He is either crazy or drunk.
他不是瘋了就是醉了。

例 He is either a student or a teacher.
他不是學生就是老師。

例 Either Tom or Tim took my book.
不是湯姆就是提姆拿走我的書。

例 Either she or you broke the window.
不是她就是你打破了玻璃。

★ Everyone knows that...

眾所皆知...

用法

完整句型為Everyone knows that S+V.這裡的know 要加s，因為everyone當作第三人稱單數，所以其 後的動詞要加s。

例句

例 Everyone knows that he likes her.
大家都知道他喜歡她。

例 Everyone knows that he is very rich.
大家都知道他非常富有。

例 Everyone knows that the news is not real.
大家都知道這消息不是真的。

例 Everyone knows that she works very hard.
大家都知道她非常努力工作。

❶ 轉折連結　❷ 表達疑問　❸ 表達情緒　❹ 表達否定　❺ 生活用語

★ For example,...

舉例來説...

用法

完整句型為 For example, S+V.而句中的 for example
也可用 for instance 替代。

例句

For example, you can choose the cheaper one.

舉例來説,你可以選擇比較便宜的東西。

For example, Tom can hand in homework on time.

舉例來説,湯姆就能準時繳交作業。

For example, exercise is a good way to lose weight.

舉例來説,運動是個不錯的減肥方式。

For example, helping people can also make you happy.

舉例來説,幫助別人也能讓你快樂。

★ For+N,...

為了...

用法

完整句型為For+N, S+V.這裡的for+N也可等於to+V(原形動詞)，皆表示"為了"。

例句

例 For his family, he works overtime every day.

為了他的家人，他每天加班工作。

例 For a better life, you should save more money.

為了更好的生活，你該多存點錢。

例 For your health, you should exercise more.

為了你的健康，你應該多運動。

例 For your future, you should study hard from now on.

為了你的將來，你現在就該好好讀書。

① 轉折連結

② 表達疑問

③ 表達情緒

④ 表達否定

⑤ 生活用語

★ from...to...

從...到...

用法

> 完整句型為S+V+ from A to B.句中的A和B為地方名稱或是時間、日期等。

例 We go to school from Monday to Friday.
我們從星期一到星期五都要上學。

例 He works from 8 a.m. to 6 p.m. every day.
他每天從早上八點工作到晚上六點。

例 They took the train from Taipei to Taichung.
他們從台北搭火車到台中。

例 She often walks from her house to that park.
她時常從她家走到那座公園。

★ Generally speaking,...

一般而言...

用法

完整句型為Generally speaking, S+V.此句型也等於In general/ Generally, S+V.

例句

例 Generally speaking, I prefer coffee to tea.
一般而言,我比較喜歡咖啡勝過茶。

例 Generally speaking, I go to work by bus.
一般而言,我都搭車去上班。

例 Generally speaking, you did well.
整體而言,你表現得很好。

例 Generally speaking, most students don't like tests.
一般而言,大部分的學生都不喜歡考試。

★ go+Ving...

從事...

用法

完整句型為S+ go+ Ving.或是S+V to+ go +Ving.
前者句中的go若用在過去式，就可改為went。

例句

例 My dad likes to go fishing.
我爸喜歡從事釣魚活動。

例 They like to go mountain climbing.
他們喜歡從事登山活動。

例 She often goes shopping with Kelly.
她常和凱莉去逛街購物。

例 We went swimming yesterday.
我們昨天去游泳。

★ He asked me...

他要求/問我...

完整句型為 He asked me to+V.或是 He asked me+
疑問詞+ S+V/to+V(原形動詞)。

例 He asked me to finish the work before tomorrow.

他要求我在明天之前完成這項工作。

例 He asked me to do him a favor.

他請我幫他一個忙。

例 He asked me how to get there.

他問我怎麼到那裡。

例 He asked me where Roy was.

他問我羅伊在哪裡。

★ He lacks...

他缺乏...

用法

完整句型為He lacks+N.其中的lack = be lacking in-be in lack of，後面都接名詞。

例句

例 He lacks money.
他缺錢。

例 He lacks patience.
他缺乏耐心。

例 He lacks courage.
他缺乏勇氣。

例 He lacks a sense of humor.
他缺乏幽默感。

★ How+Adj....

...是多麼...

用法

完整句型為How+Adj.+S+V.此種句型的how是當作"多麼"之意,有強調語氣的成分。

例句

🔘 How beautiful the girl is!
那個女孩是多麼美呀!

🔘 How cute the puppy is!
那隻小狗多麼可愛呀!

🔘 How big that house is!
那間房子是多麼的大!

🔘 How sad she looks!
她看起來是多麼悲傷!

★ Hundreds of...

數以百計的...

完整句型為 Hundreds of+S+V. 句中的主詞必為複數名詞，須特別注意。

例 Hundreds of people joined that activity.
數以百計的群眾參加了那場活動。

例 Hundreds of people died in the earthquake.
數以百計的人們在那次地震喪生。

例 Hundreds of passengers go to work by MRT.
數以百計的乘客搭捷運上班。

例 Hundreds of students didn't pass the exam.
數以百計的學生沒有通過考試。

★ I believe that...

我相信...

用法

完整句型為 I believe that S+V. 句中的 believe 若改為 trust(相信)，句型則為 A+ trust + that S+V，與 believe 用法不同。若要說 "我不相信"，則是 I don't believe that...，不可將 not 置於 that 子句中。

例句

例 I believe that you can make it.
我相信你可以做得到的。

例 I believe that she is innocent.
我相信她是無辜的。

例 I believe that we can win the game.
我相信我們可以贏得這場比賽。

例 I believe that he can succeed.
我相信他可以成功。

★ I forgot...

我忘記...

完整句型為 I forgot+N./I forgot to+V(原形動詞)./
I forgot+Ving.這三種句型中,第一種指單純忘記
某人或事物。而 forgot to+V 是指"忘記去做某
事"。forgot+Ving 則是"忘記做過某事"。forgot
的原形為 forget。

例 Sorry. I forgot your name.
抱歉,我忘了你的名字。

例 I forgot to bring my key.
我忘了帶鑰匙。

例 I forgot to mail the letter.
我忘了寄信。

例 I forgot mailing the letter.
信寄了,我卻忘了。

★ I found...

我發現/覺...

完整句型為I found thatS+V.或是I found+N.句中的found原形為find，而find又等於discover，兩者用法相同。

例 I found your book.
　　我找到了你的書。

例 I found a secret place.
　　我發現了一個神祕的地方。

例 I found that the question was difficult.
　　我發現這問題是困難的。

例 I found that Henry likes Mary.
　　我發現亨利喜歡瑪莉。

★ I have a question...

> 我有問題...

完整句型為 I have a question about+N.或是 I have a question to+V(原形動詞)。

例 I have a question to ask you.
我有問題要問你。

例 I have a question about the plan.
關於這項計畫，我有疑問。

例 I have a question about the case.
關於這個案子，我有疑問。

例 I have a question about the answer.
關於這個答案，我有疑問。

★ I heard that...

我聽説...

完整句型為 I heard that S+V. 句中的 heard，其原
形為 hear。句中的 hear 不可用 listen 替代，因為用
法不同，listen 通常與 to 連用，或單一使用。例
如：Listen!(聽！)或是 listen to music(聽音樂)。

例 I heard that she was ill.
我聽説她生病了。

例 I heard that she quit.
我聽説她辭職了。

例 I heard that he went to Taipei.
我聽説他去台北了。

例 I heard that he got married.
我聽説他結婚了。

❶ 轉折連結　❷ 表達疑問　❸ 表達情緒　❹ 表達否定　❺ 生活用語

★ I insist...

我堅持...

用法

完整句型為 I insist on+N./ I insist on+Ving./ I insist that S+V.句中的insist on=persist in。

例句

例 I insist on this decision.
我堅持這個決定。

例 I insist on seeing it.
我一定要看到它。

例 He insisted that she was wrong.
他堅持她是錯的。

例 He insisted that he didn't do it.
他堅持他沒這麼做。

★ I know...

> 我知道...

用法

> 完整句型為I know+N.或是I know that S+V.抑或
> 是I know+疑問詞+to+V(原形動詞)。

例句

例 I know him.
　　我知道他。

例 I know you.
　　我了解你。

例 I know how to do it.
　　我知道該怎麼做。

例 I know when to leave.
　　我知道何時該離開。

★ I make it a rule to...

我養成...習慣

用法

完整句型為I make it a rule to +V(原形動詞).其中的rule可用habit或是custom替代。

例句

例 I make it a rule to get up early.
我養成早起的習慣。

例 I make it a rule to study English every day.
我養成每天讀英文的習慣。

例 I make it a rule to exercise every Friday.
我養成每週五運動的習慣。

例 I make it a rule to brush my teeth every day.
我養成每天刷牙的習慣。

★ I recommend...

我推薦/建議....

完整句型為I recommend+N. / I recommend that S+(should)+V(原形動詞).這裡的動詞要用原形動詞，因為習慣上會省略掉should，所以後面動詞會用原形動詞。

例句

📗 I recommend this movie.
我推薦這部電影。

📗 I recommend that restaurant.
我推薦那間餐廳。

📗 I recommend you leave now.
我建議你現在離開。

📗 I recommend you follow the rules.
我建議你遵守這些規則。

★ I said that...

我說...

完整句型為 I said that S+V.句中的 said，其原形
為 say。

例 I said that I love you.
我說我愛你。

例 I said that we should leave.
我說我們該走了。

例 I said that we should go home.
我說我們回家吧。

例 I said that it was not true.
我說那不是真的。

★ I saw...

我看見...

用法

完整句型為 I saw+N.或是 I saw +A+Ving.抑或 I saw that S+V.句中 saw 的原形為 see。此句的 see 不能用 look 替代,因為 look 常與 at 連用,或是單獨使用。

例句

例 I saw her yesterday.
我昨天有看到她。

例 I saw him crying.
我看見他在哭。

例 I saw Tom talking to Jack.
我看見湯姆在跟傑克講話。

例 I saw you do it.
我看見是你做的。

★I suggest that...

我建議...

用法

完整句型為 I suggest that S+(should)+V(原形動詞).句中的動詞要用原形動詞,因為習慣上會省略掉should,所以後面動詞會用原形動詞。

例句

例 I suggest that you eat less.
我建議你少吃一點。

例 I suggest that you exercise more.
我建議你多運動。

例 I suggest that you see a doctor.
我建議你去看醫生。

例 I suggest that you study English every day.
我建議你每天讀英文。

★ I think that...

我認為...

用法

完整句型為 I think (that) S+V.若要說 "我不認為",則為 I don't think that... 。不可以將 not 放於 that 子句中,例如:I think that I don't....(×)

例句

例 I think that she will come.
我認為她會來。

例 I think he will win the game.
我認為他會贏得這場比賽。

例 I think that you will succeed.
我認為你會成功。

例 I think that you will pass the exam.
我認為你會通過這考試。

① 轉折連結 ② 表達疑問 ③ 表達情緒 ④ 表達否定 ⑤ 生活用語

251 🎧 track 5-34

★ I want...

我想...

用法

完整句型為I want +N.或為I want to+V(原形動詞)。而want也可等於would like,後面都接to+V(原形動詞)。

例句

例 I want this one.
我想要這一個。

例 I want that job.
我想要那份工作。

例 I want to go home.
我想要回家。

例 I want to see a movie.
我想看電影。

★ I wish...

> 我希望...

用法

完整句型為I wish+ S+ Vpt(過去式動詞).→與現在事實相反。或是I wish+ S+had Vpp.(過去完成式)→與過去事實相反。所以上述兩種句型皆為假設語氣。

例句

- I wish I could see her again.
  我希望我可以再見到她。

- I wish I knew more people.
  我希望我認識更多人。

- I wish I were a rich man.
  我希望我是有錢人。

- I wish I didn't have to work.
  我希望我不用工作。

❷ ❽ ❺

① 轉折連結

② 表達疑問

③ 表達情緒

④ 表達否定

⑤ 生活用語

★ I'm on the way to...

我在...路上

完整句型為I'm on the way to+地點.此句意表示
正在往某處前進或在路上之意。另外若要說回家
的話，則可將the改成所有格，例如：my, his, her
等。但主詞也要隨其變動，且不加to，如：I'm on
my way home. (我在回家的路上。)

例 I'm on the way to school.
我在去上學的路上。

例 I'm on the way to work.
我在去上班的路上。

例 I'm on the way to Taipei.
我在去台北的路上。

例 I'm on the way to his home.
我在去他家的路上。

★ I'm surprised...

我很驚訝...

用法

完整句型為I'm surprised that S+V.或是I'm surprised at+N./ I'm surprised to+V(原形動詞).若為過去式，be動詞也要跟著改。

例句

例 I'm surprised at the news.
我很驚訝這個消息。

例 I'm surprised at his decision.
我對他的決定感到驚訝。

例 I was surprised to learn the news.
我很驚訝知道這個消息。

例 I was surprised that he passed the exam.
我很驚訝他通過考試。

❶轉折連結 ❷表達疑問 ❸表達情緒 ❹表達否定 ❺生活用語

英語句型 這樣學才會快

★ I'm willing to...

我願意...

用法

完整句型為I'm willing to +V(原形動詞).當你想釋出善意或自願想幫助對方,或是對方需要協助時,就可用此句型來表達。

例句

例 I'm willing to help you.
我願意幫你。

例 I'm willing to come.
我願意來。

例 I'm willing to do the work.
我願意做這項工作。

例 I'm willing to stay here.
我願意待在這裡。

★ In my opinion,...

依我所見...

 用法

完整句型為 In my opinion, S+V.=As far as I'm concerned, S+V.

 例句

例 In my opinion, the answer is wrong.
依我之見，這答案有錯。

例 In my opinion, the price is reasonable.
依我之見，這價錢還算合理。

例 In my opinion, he may lose the game.
依我之見，他可能會輸掉這場比賽。

例 In my opinion, it's not easy to do the work.
依我之見，這工作沒那麼好做。

❶ 轉折連結

❷ 表達疑問

❸ 表達情緒

❹ 表達否定

❺ 生活用語

★ including+N...

包含...

完整句型為S+V, including+N.此句型也等於S+V, inclusive of+N.而include為原形動詞，inclusive則是形容詞。

例 I love fast food, including pizza.
我愛速食，包括披薩。

例 I like her, including her family.
我喜歡她，包含她的家人。

例 They all died, including his son.
他們都死了，包括他的兒子。

例 They moved, including John.
他們都搬走了，包括約翰。

★ It could be...

有可能...

用法

完整句型為It could be+N/Adj,此句意只是當事人的猜測,並非百分之百的確定。

例句

例 It could be you.
那有可能是你。

例 It could be mine.
那有可能是我的。

例 It could be true.
那有可能是真的。

例 It could be dangerous.
那有可能很危險。

★ It goes without saying that...

不用說...

完整句型為 It goes without saying that S+V. 此句型也等於 It is needless to say that S+V.

例 It goes without saying that he can pass the test.
不用說也知道，他一定會及格的。

例 It goes without saying that he can succeed.
不用說也知道，他一定會成功的。

例 It goes without saying that she will win the game.
不用說也知道，她會獲勝。

例 It goes without saying that she likes him.
不用說也知道，她喜歡他。

★ It is +Adj.+ enough...

...已足夠

用法

完整句型為It is+Adj.+ enough to +V(原形動詞)/ for +N.當對方對於某事物已覺得滿足時，就可以用此句型。

例句

⑩ It is big enough for me.
它對我來說夠大了。

⑩ It is good enough for you.
它對你來說夠好了。

⑩ It is easy enough to do the work.
這工作已經夠簡單了。

⑩ It is hard enough to make a living.
謀生已經夠難了。

★ It is quite...

...很；蠻...

用法

完整句型為 It is quite+Adj. 句中的 quite 有時候也可以用 very，不過 very 的語氣較強烈或是肯定，因其表示"非常"之意。

例句

例 It is quite easy.
它還蠻簡單的。

例 It is quite hard.
它還蠻困難的。

例 It is quite small.
它還蠻小的。

例 It is quite cute.
它還蠻可愛的。

★ It is said that...

據說...

完整句型為It is said that S+V.而 it is said=people say=they say.其用法也相同。

📖 It is said that he is going to quit.
據說他打算要辭職。

📖 It is said that she is pregnant.
據說她懷孕了。

📖 It is said that the news is true.
據說這消息是真的。

📖 It is said that they live in Taipei.
據說他們現在住在台北。

★ It is time for you to...

你該...

完整句型為It is time for you to+V(原形動詞)。此
句意為提醒或建議對方該做某事了。句中的It is
time表示 "是時候" 之意。

例 It is time for you to go to bed.

你該去睡覺了。

例 It is time for you to get up.

你該起床了。

例 It is time for you to do homework.

你該寫功課了。

例 It is time for you to go home.

你該回家了。

★ It is+Ving/Adj....

...很...

用法

完整句型為It is +Ving./ It is Adj.此句型是用來
表示當下的情境或當事人對某事物的感覺,但也
有可能是事實的描述。

例句

例 It is cute.

它真可愛。

例 It is interesting.

這真有趣。

例 It is boring.

這真無聊。

例 It is raining outside.

外面正在下雨。

★ It looks like...

它看起來好像...

用法

完整句型為 It looks like+N. 或是 It looks like+(that) S+V.這裡的 like 是介系詞，表示 "像..." 之意，而非一般動詞 "喜歡"。

例句

例 It looks like rain.

好像要下雨了。

例 It looks like a picture.

它看起來好像一幅畫。

例 It looks like you like her.

看起來你好像喜歡她。

例 It looks like you're having dinner.

看起來你好像在吃晚餐。

★ It occurred to me...

我忽然想到...

用法

完整句型為 It occurred to me that S+V./ It occurred to me to+V(原形動詞).這裡的 occur 不能用 think 替代，it occurred to+人是習慣用語。

例句

⬤ It occurred to me to visit my teacher.
我想去拜訪老師。

⬤ It occurred to me to buy clothes.
我想去買衣服。

⬤ It occurred to me that I forgot to bring my key.
我忽然想到我忘了帶鑰匙。

⬤ It occurred to me that I haven't finished my homework.
我忽然想到我還沒完成我的功課。

轉折連結 ❶ 表達疑問 ❷ 表達情緒 ❸ 表達否定 ❹ 生活用語 ❺

★ It seems that...

它似乎...

完整句型為It seems that S+V.這裡的seem也可用
appear(有似乎、出現之意)替代。

例 It seems that the train has gone.
火車似乎已經開走了。

例 It seems that you have finished the work.
你似乎已經完成這個工作。

例 It seems that he has left.
他似乎已經走了。

例 It seems that you like her very much.
你似乎很喜歡她。

★ It will be...

它將會是...

用法

> 完整句型為It will be+Adj./N.這裡的will be是未
> 來式,所以只是當事人的期望,不代表現況。

例句

🔘 It will be all right.
　那將會沒事的。

🔘 It will be fun.
　那將會很有趣。

🔘 It will be mine.
　那將會是我的。

🔘 It will be a problem.
　那將會是個問題。

★ It's estimated that...

據估計...

用法

完整句型為 It's estimated that S+V. 而 estimated 的原形為 estimate。

例句

例 It's estimated that the typhoon is coming tomorrow.

據估計,颱風明天將會來。

例 It's estimated that they may cancel the game.

據估計,他們可能取消這次比賽。

例 It's estimated that only 15 students passed the exam.

據估計,只有15位學生通過考試。

例 It's estimated that 20 people died in the fire.

據估計有二十人死於那場火災。

★ It's hard to...

...很難...

用法

完整句型為 It's hard to +V(原形動詞).而 hard 當
"困難的" 之意時，可等於 difficult。

例句

📖 It's hard to say.

這很難說。

📖 It's hard to say goodbye.

很難說再見。

📖 It's hard to do the work.

這工作很難做。

📖 It's hard to answer the question.

這問題很難回答。

★ It's likely...

有可能...

完整句型為 It's likely to+V(原形動詞).或是 It's likely that S+V.

例 It's likely to be true.
有可能是真的。

例 It's likely to be serious.
有可能很嚴重。

例 It's likely that she will move.
她有可能搬家。

例 It's likely that he won't come.
他有可能不會來。

★ It's time to...

該是...的時間

用法

完整句型為It's time to+V(原形動詞).當你覺得對方該做某事的時候，就可用此句型來建議或勸告之。

例句

例 It's time to stop.
該停止了。

例 It's time to change.
該改變了。

例 It's time to go.
該走了。

例 It's time to say goodbye.
該說再見了。

❶轉折連結 ❷表達疑問 ❸表達情緒 ❹表達否定 ❺生活用語

★ I've decided to...

我已決定...

用法

完整句型為 I've decided to +V(原形動詞).因為是已經決定,且有要去實踐的行動,所以用現在完成式。若單純用 decided(過去式),則表示是之前所做下的決定。

例句

例 I've decided to quit.
我已決定要辭職。

例 I've decided to move.
我已決定要搬家。

例 I've decided to go abroad.
我已決定要出國。

例 I've decided to marry him.
我已決定要嫁給他。

★ Let me...

讓我...

用法

完整句型為Let me+ V(原形動詞).由於let為使役動詞，所以其後的動詞為原形動詞，不加to。

例句

例 Let me go.
讓我走吧。

例 Let me do it.
讓我來做這件事吧。

例 Let me help you.
讓我來幫你吧。

例 Let me show you.
讓我來示範一次給你看吧。

❶ 轉折連結

❷ 表達疑問

❸ 表達情緒

❹ 表達否定

❺ 生活用語

★ Many people...

許多人...

用法

完整句型為Many people+V.這裡的動詞時態可為
現在式、過去式或完成式，視說話者所欲表達之
意。但是要注意，若為現在式或現在完成式，動
詞須用複數形。

例句

例 Many people like the singer.
許多人喜歡那位歌手。

例 Many people want to be rich.
許多人想要致富。

例 Many people died in the earthquake.
許多人死於那場地震中。

例 Many people joined the activity.
許多人參加那場活動。

★ mistake A for B...

誤以為 A 是 B...

完整句型為 S+ mistake A for B.這裡的 mistake 不是當 "錯誤" 解，是動詞，而非名詞。若是過去式，則用 mistook。

例 I mistook that girl for Helen.
我誤以為那個女生是海倫。

例 I mistook this man for your dad.
我誤以為這個人是你爸。

例 I mistook the book for mine.
我誤以為這本書是我的。

例 I mistook the cell phone for yours.
我誤以為這手機是你的。

★ Most/Most of the...

大部分的...

用法

完整句型為 Most+N+V. 或是 Most of the+N+V. 句型中的 N 為複數名詞，而動詞也是複數形。

例句

例 Most people like the movie.
大部分的人都喜歡這部電影。

例 Most students don't like tests.
大部分的學生都不喜歡考試。

例 Most of the books are not mine.
這大部分的書都不是我的。

例 Most parents love their children.
大部分的家長都愛他們的小孩。

★ My dream is to...

我的夢想是...

完整句型為My dream is to+V(原形動詞)。這裡的 is to+V有未來式之意，因為尚未達成，所以用 to+V。

例 My dream is to be a doctor.
我的夢想是成為一位醫生。

例 My dream is to be a rich man
我的夢想是當個有錢人。

例 My dream is to travel around the world.
我的夢想是環遊世界。

例 My dream is to help people.
我的夢想就是幫助人們。

★ My hobby is...

我的嗜好是...

完整句型為 My hobby is+Ving/N.這裡不可用 My hobby is to+V，因為嗜好是個既有的事實或為一種持續的狀態，所以用 Ving。

例 My hobby is reading.
我的嗜好是閱讀。

例 My hobby is singing.
我的嗜好是唱歌。

例 My hobby is playing basketball.
我的嗜好是打籃球。

例 My hobby is listening to music.
我的嗜好是聽音樂。

★ One of the...

其中...

完整句型為 One of the+N+V. 此句型中的N為複數名詞，而動詞則為單數形，因為主詞是 one。若為過去式，動詞則不受主詞影響，皆為過去式。

例 One of the boys is my brother.
　其中一個男生是我的弟弟。

例 One of the movies is my favorite.
　其中一部電影是我的最愛。

例 One of the books is mine.
　其中有一本書是我的。

例 One of the men left.
　其中有一個人走了。

① 轉折連結
② 表達疑問
③ 表達情緒
④ 表達否定
⑤ 生活用語

★ Please+V...

請...

用法

完整句型為Please+V(原形動詞).此為特定用法，
因為此句中的please有請求或命令之意，即為祈
使句，所以動詞要用原形動詞。主詞則是省略掉
的you(習慣用法)。

例句

例 Please wait.
請等一下。

例 Please go home.
請你回家。

例 Please answer me.
請你回答我。

例 Please open the door.
請打開門。

★ regard A as B...

認為 A 為 B...

用法

| 完整句型為S+regard A as B.=S +think of A as B. |

例句

例 I regard you as my family.
我視你為我的家人。

例 I regard him as my brother.
我把他當作兄弟。

例 I regard him as a genius.
我認為他是天才。

例 I regard her as my best friend.
我視她為我最好的朋友。

283

★ rid oneself of...

戒除...

用法

完整句型為S+V+to+rid oneself of+N/Ving.或是S+ rid oneself of+N/Ving.

例句

📖 I try to rid myself of him.
我試著忘掉他。

📖 He couldn't rid himself of the girl.
他無法忘掉那個女生。

📖 It's hard to rid oneself of a bad habit.
要戒除掉壞習慣是困難的。

📖 She wants to rid herself of the noisy kid.
她想擺脫掉那個煩人的小鬼。

★ S+V by oneself...

...獨自...

完整句型為S+V by oneself.句中的by oneself=on one's own。

例 I did the work by myself.
我獨自做這工作。

例 She cooked dinner by herself.
她一個人煮晚餐。

例 He went there by himself.
他獨自一人去那裡。

例 He finished the report by himself.
他獨自完成這份報告。

❶ 轉折連結

❷ 表達疑問

❸ 表達情緒

❹ 表達否定

❺ 生活用語

★ S+V during...

在...期間...

用法

完整句型為S+V during+N.句中的during須接時間名詞,例如:during Christmas(在聖誕節期間)、during July(在七月期間)。

例句

例 She finished the work during the week.
她在一週內完成這項工作。

例 She often exercises during the weekend.
她常在週末運動。

例 She visited Kelly during the winter break.
她在寒假期間去拜訪凱莉。

例 She went abroad during the summer vacation.
她在暑假期間出國。

★ S+V in the future...

未來...

用法

完整句型為S+V in the future.或是In the future, S+V.

例句

例 I want to be a boss in the future.
我以後要當老闆。

例 I want to buy a house in the future.
我以後要買一間房子。

例 I have confidence in the future.
我對未來有信心。

例 I will succeed one day in the future.
未來總有一天我會成功。

★ So far,...

目前為止...

 用法

完整句型為 So far, S+V. 由於 so far 表示 "從過去到現在為止的一段時間"，因此常與現在完成式合用。

 例句

例 So far, I haven't seen anyone.

到目前為止，我還沒見到任何一個人。

例 So far, I haven't heard from him.

到目前為止，我還沒收到他的信。

例 So far, no one has had his news.

到目前為止，沒人有他的消息。

例 So far, the police haven't found the boy.

到目前為止，警方還是找不到那個男生。

★ Someone told me that...

有人告訴我...

完整句型為Someone told me that S+V.這裡told 的原形為tell。而tell+人，talk to+人，兩者用法 不同。

例 Someone told me that I should stop.
有人告訴我，我該停止了。

例 Someone told me that I should relax.
有人告訴我，我該放鬆一下。

例 Someone told me that I need to take a rest.
有人告訴我，我需要休息一下。

例 Someone told me that I have to see a doctor.
有人告訴我，我必須去看醫生。

289

🎧 track 5-53

★ something+Adj....

事情有些...

用法

完整句型為S+V+something+Adj./ 助V(助動詞)+ S+V+ something+Adj.?(疑問句)。所以此句型用於肯定句或是否定句皆可。

例句

例 I found something weird.

我發現事情有些詭異。

例 I have something good for you.

我有不錯的東西要給你。

例 Can I have something to eat?

我可以吃點什麼東西嗎？

例 Do you know something special?

你知道有什麼新鮮事嗎？

★ Speaking of...

說到...

用法

完整句型為Speaking of+N/Ving, S+V.或是
Speaking of+N/Ving, 助V(助動詞)+S+V?
所以speaking of後面可接一個完整的肯定句或是
否定句。

例句

例 Speaking of him, I'm getting angry.
說到他,我就怒火中燒。

例 Speaking of Kevin, I met him yesterday.
說到凱文,我昨天有遇到他。

例 Speaking of food, do you like pizza?
說到食物,你喜歡披薩嗎?

例 Speaking of the plan, do you have any idea?
說到這個計畫,你有任何想法嗎?

★ stop A from...

阻止/禁止 A...

 用法

完整句型為S+ stop A from+Ving. 句中的stop也可以用keep替代。

 例句

🔢 She stopped me from going to the party.
她阻止我去參加舞會。

🔢 He stopped me from seeing a movie.
他阻止我去看電影。

🔢 My mom stopped me from watching TV.
我媽禁止我看電視。

🔢 My dad stopped me from going out at night.
我爸禁止我晚上外出。

★ take your time...

慢慢做...

用法

> 完整句型為 Take your time+Ving. 或是 S+助 V(助動詞)+take your time+Ving.

例句

🔘 Take your time doing the work.
你慢慢做這份工作吧。

🔘 Take your time enjoying this trip.
慢慢來,好好享受這趟旅程吧。

🔘 You can take your time doing it.
你可以慢慢地來做這件事。

🔘 You should take your time tasting the food.
你應該從容不迫地好好品嘗這食物。

❸
❷
❺

❶ 轉折連結

❷ 表達疑問

❸ 表達情緒

❹ 表達否定

❺ 生活用語

★ Tell me how...

告訴我...如何...

完整句型為 Tell me how S+V. 或是 Tell me how to+V(原形動詞).

例 Tell me how you feel now.
　　告訴我你現在感覺如何。

例 Tell me how he made it.
　　告訴我他如何做到的。

例 Tell me how to do it.
　　告訴我怎麼做這事。

例 Tell me how to study English.
　　告訴我該如何念英文。

★ That should be...

那應該是...

用法

完整句型為 That should be +Adj./N. 此句型常用在
當事人對某件事,持有主觀的猜測或看法,但事
實結果不一定如其所想。

例句

例 That should be real.
那應該是真的。

例 That should be wrong.
那應該是錯的。

例 That should be him.
那應該是他。

例 That should be Allen.
那應該是艾倫。

★ The access to...

通往...的途徑

完整句型為 The access to+N+V.或是 S+V+the access to+N.

例 The access to the exit is here.
通往出口的路在這裡。

例 The access to success is working hard.
通往成功的途徑就是努力工作。

例 I know the access to that place.
我知道通往那個地方的路。

例 I can't find the access to the store.
我找不到往那家店的路。

★ the+...est/the most...

最...

完整句型為S+V+ the+...est(最高級形容詞)/the
most+Adj.+N.句中the+最高級形容詞的用法，須
用在對象為三者以上的情況。

例 He is the tallest boy in the class.
他是班上最高的男生。

例 He is the best man I know.
他是我所認識的人裡，最好的人。

例 She is the most beautiful girl I've ever met.
她是我遇過最美麗的女生。

例 This is the happiest moment I've ever had.
這是我有過最快樂的時光。

★ There is/are...

有...

完整句型為There is/are+N.或是There is/are+Ving. 句中的there is和there are皆表示"有"的意思， 不同之處在於：there is+單數可數名詞或是不可數名詞皆可；而there are+複數可數名詞。

例 There is nothing to say.
　沒什麼好說的。

例 There is a car behind you.
　你身後有一輛車子。

例 There is a girl crying.
　有一個女生在哭。

例 There are four people in my family.
　我家有四個人。

★ There must be...

一定有...

用法

完整句型為There must be+N.句中的there be就是
"有"的意思。而must則表示"一定",所以此
句型是一種強調的語氣,表示當事人對某件事有
個堅定的看法,但結果是否真如其所想,就不一
定了。

例句

例 There must be a way out.
　一定有辦法解決的。

例 There must be a misunderstanding.
　這一定有誤會。

例 There must be an answer to the question.
　這問題一定有答案的。

例 There must be something wrong with the
　case.
　這案件一定有問題。

299

★ There seems to be...

似乎有...

完整句型為 There seems to be+N+(Ving).若要說 "似乎沒有",句型則為 There doesn't seem to be+N(Ving).

例 There seems to be good news.
似乎有好消息。

例 There seems to be nothing special.
似乎沒什麼特別的。

例 There seems to be a man watching us.
似乎有人在看我們。

例 There seems to be a stranger following you.
似乎有一個陌生人跟著你。

★ There used to be...

曾經有...

完整句型為There used to be+N.句中的used to為
過去式，表示曾經有過的，但現在已沒有。而
there be則為"有"的意思。

例 There used to be a school here.
　這裡曾經有一所學校。

例 There used to be a hospital there.
　那裡曾經有一間醫院。

例 There used to be a dog in my home.
　我家曾經有養一隻狗。

例 There used to be a park near my house.
　我家附近曾經有一座公園。

301

★ There will be...

將會有...

用法

完整句型為There will be+N+(Ving). 此句型屬於未來式。句中的N可為複數名詞，或是單數可數名詞、不可數名詞；而動詞加ing則是因為有be。

例句

例 There will be rain tomorrow.
明天將會下雨。

例 There will be a typhoon next Monday.
下週一將會有颱風。

例 There will be more people coming here.
將會有更多人來這裡。

例 There will be many students joining the game.
將會有許多學生參加這次的比賽。

★ This is the only...

這是唯一...

完整句型為This is the only +N that S+V.句中的 that 可以省略，不會影響句意。而既然是 the only，所以後面接的名詞須為單數可數名詞。

例 This is the only thing I have.
這是我唯一所擁有的。

例 This is the only thing I can do.
這是唯一我能做的。

例 This is the only way we can leave.
這是唯一我們能離開的方法。

例 This is the only way we can save her.
這是唯一我們能救她的方法。

★ To+V...

為了...

用法

完整句型為To+V(原形動詞), S+V.句中的to+V是
一種表達「為了達到某個目的」之意，因此用to+
V，與for+N(為了...)意思相同，但用法不同。

例句

例 To succeed, I work hard.

為了成功，我努力工作。

例 To save time, I take the MRT to work.

為了節省時間，我搭捷運上班。

例 To lose weight, I exercise every day.

為了減肥，我每天運動。

例 To win the game, I practice every day.

為了贏得比賽，我每天練習。

★ too...to...

太...以至於不能...

完整句型為S+ beV+ too+ Adj.+ to + V(原形動詞).=S+V+so+Adj./Adv.+that+否定子句.

例句

例 He is too young to go to school.
他太小還不能去上學。

例 He is too old to work.
他太老無法工作。

例 The question is too hard to understand.
這問題太難，無法理解。

例 The wind is too strong to go out.
風太強無法出門。

❶轉折連結　❷表達疑問　❸表達情緒　❹表達否定　❺生活用語

★ When it comes to...

談到...

用法

完整句型為When it comes to+N/Ving, S+V.其實
when it comes to就等於speaking of，用法也相
同，後面都可接一個完整的肯定句或疑問句。

例句

例 When it comes to exams, I feel stressed.
談到考試，我就感到壓力。

例 When it comes to the accident, I feel sad.
談到那個意外，我就感到難過。

例 When it comes to sports, do you like baseball?
談到運動，你喜歡棒球嗎？

例 When it comes to traveling, which place do you like?
說到旅行，你喜歡哪一個地方？

★ With+N,...

因為(有)...

完整句型為With+N, S+V.這裡的 with 可以當作 "因為、有、儘管" 等意思解，所以其句意需要 視上下文或說話者所要表達之意而定。

例 With her support, I could make it.
有她的支持，我才能成功。

例 With her help, I passed the test.
有她的幫忙，我才得以通過考試。

例 With rain, we didn't go out.
因為下雨，所以我們沒有出門。

例 With failure, she didn't give up.
儘管失敗，她並沒有放棄。

307　　　　　　　　　　🎧 track 5-62

★ Without doubt,...

毫無疑問

用法

完整句型為 Without doubt, S+V. 而 without doubt=
without question=doubtless，用法皆相同。

例
句

例 Without doubt, he is the best.
毫無疑問，他是最棒的。

例 Without doubt, he is the one.
毫無疑問，他就是我的真愛。

例 Without doubt, no one likes him.
毫無疑問，沒有人喜歡他。

例 Without doubt, he works very hard.
毫無疑問，他工作非常認真。

★ You can...

你可以...

完整句型為You can+V(原形動詞).當 "可以" 或 "能夠" 之意時,也能用could(can的過去式)代替,且could的語氣較委婉。

例 You can make it.
你可以的。

例 You can trust me.
你可以相信我。

例 You can go home.
你可以回家了。

例 You can start now.
你現在可以開始了。

英語句型 這樣學才會快

★ You may...

你可能/可以...

用法

完整句型為 You may+V(原形動詞).而 may 也可用 might(may的過去式)替代,只是 might 的語氣較委 婉。若 m 大寫,則表示"五月"(May)之意,也可 為人名。

例句

例 You may call me.
你可以打給我。

例 You may come in.
你可以進來。

例 You may check it again.
你可能要再檢查一次。

例 You may show her how to do it.
你可能要示範一次怎麼做給她看。

★ You should...

你應該...

 用法

完整句型為You should+V(原形動詞).=You ought to+ V(原形動詞).=You are supposed to+ V(原形動詞).

 例句

📙 You should go home.
你該回家了。

📙 You should take a rest.
你該休息一下。

📙 You should stop.
你該停止了。

📙 You should try again.
你應該再試一次。

★ You'd better...

你最好...

完整句型為 You'd better+V(原形動詞).而 You'd=
You had。若為否定句，句型則為 You'd better not+
V(原形動詞).不可寫為 better not to+V(×)

例 You'd better leave.
你最好離開。

例 You'd better stay here.
你最好待在這裡。

例 You'd better not touch it.
你最好別碰它。

例 You'd better not go out.
你最好別出去。

★ You have to...

你必須...

完整句型為You have to +V(原形動詞).此句型常
用在不得已的情況下，所要完成的行為或任務。

📖 You have to go now.
你現在必須離開。

📖 You have to finish it.
你必須把它完成。

📖 You have to trust me.
你必須相信我。

📖 You have to get used to it.
你必須習慣它。

★ You will...

你將會...

用法

完整句型為 You will+V(原形動詞). 此句型常用於鼓勵、提醒、或告知對方,做或不做某事情時,或是某事情未來的發展,可能會有什麼樣的結果之情形。

例句

例 You will be fine.
你會沒事的。

例 You will know it.
你會知道的。

例 You will succeed one day.
總有一天你會成功的。

例 You will see her next time.
下次你就能見到她。

★ You owe...

你欠...

完整句型為 You owe+人(受詞)+N. 此句中的受詞可為 me,him,her,them,us 或人名等，而 N 則可為單數可數名詞、不可數名詞或是複數可數名詞。

例 You owe me money.
你欠我錢。

例 You owe me a meal.
你欠我一餐。

例 You owe me an apology.
你欠我一個道歉。

例 You owe him a lot.
你虧欠他許多。

永續圖書
線上購物網

www.foreverbooks.com.tw

◆ 加入會員即享活動及會員折扣。

◆ 每月均有優惠活動，期期不同。

◆ 新加入會員三天內訂購書籍不限本數金額，
   即贈送精選書籍一本。（依網站標示為主）

專業圖書發行、書局經銷、圖書出版

英語句型這樣學才會快

雅致風靡　典藏文化

親愛的顧客您好，感謝您購買這本書。即日起，填寫讀者回函卡寄回至
本公司，我們每月將抽出一百名回函讀者，寄出精美禮物並享有生日當
月購書優惠！想知道更多更即時的消息，歡迎加入"永續圖書粉絲團"
您也可以選擇傳真、掃描或用本公司準備的免郵回函寄回，謝謝。

傳真電話：（02）8647-3660　　　　電子信箱：yungjiuh@ms45.hinet.net

姓名：		性別：	□男　　□女
出生日期：　年　　月　　日		電話：	
學歷：		職業：	
E-mail：			
地址：□□□			
從何處購買此書：		購買金額：	元
購買本書動機：□封面 □書名 □排版 □內容 □作者 □偶然衝動			
你對本書的意見： 內容：□滿意□尚可□待改進　　編輯：□滿意□尚可□待改進 封面：□滿意□尚可□待改進　　定價：□滿意□尚可□待改進			
其他建議：			

總經銷：永續圖書有限公司

永續圖書線上購物網
www.foreverbooks.com.tw

您可以使用以下方式將回函寄回。

您的回覆，是我們進步的最大動力，謝謝。

① 使用本公司準備的免郵回函寄回。

② 傳真電話：（02）8647-3660

③ 掃描圖檔寄到電子信箱：

　yungjiuh@ms45.hinet.net

沿此線對折後寄回，謝謝。

2 2 1 - 0 3

 雅典文化事業有限公司　收

新北市汐止區大同路三段194號9樓之1

雅致風靡　典藏文化